Liasies

by BRAXTON TYLER

Order this book online at www.trafford.com
or email orders@trafford.com

Most Trafford titles are also available at major online book retailers.

Printed in the United States of America.

Library of Congress Control Number: 2011907458

ISBN: 978-1-4269-6407-7

Trafford rev. 05/10/2011

www.trafford.com

North America & international
toll-free: 1 888 232 4444 (USA & Canada)
phone: 250 383 6864 ✦ fax: 812 355 4082

Chickery awoke to the annoying sound of his alarm clock on Monday morning, and he groaned out loud to himself when he quickly realized that he was now disturbed from what was a beautiful sleep. See, little Chickery loved to sleep, perhaps more so than his brothers, and so it wasn't surprising that he felt very annoyed in being woken up by his stupid alarm clock.

Although this had happened many times in the past, today was Monday, and that made him more annoyed than anything in the world.

Chickery was enjoying his wonderful sleep, but now he was startled and awake, and he could feel the hot heat of the morning sun shining very brightly through his bedroom window and he realized then that he was starting to sweat since his entire body was positioned in the bright sunlight.

Chickery rolled over to the side and buried his face against his pillow.

What was today? He wondered to himself. Monday? Wednesday? He had no idea.

It couldn't be a Monday since it didn't feel like Monday.

But he knew either way, it was definitely not the weekend and so that meant he had to get up and go to school and he groaned.

Great, just about the most three things he hated more than anything in his life.

The hot summer's heat, school and that stupid alarm clock, which at this moment seem to be teasing him, perhaps it was alive and it was trying to make him angrier because it kept on beeping louder by the second.

Feeling frustrated, he knocked the clock to the floor and felt very pleased with himself when he heard nothing but silence and while he smiled in satisfaction, he rolled over and tried to sleep.

School can wait, in the meantime he is going to try to get another 10 minutes of sleep.

Too late. He heard loud footsteps pounding up the staircase and he groaned out loud.

He recognized the sound of those footsteps.

"Morning, up there! Rise and shine! You better get up or you will be late for school!"

Chickery groaned out loud to himself and buried his face deeper into his pillow. He has always hated Monday mornings and today was no different.

He dreaded waking up and having to deal with the loud noise that always seems to be present

Inside his household since deep down he personally thought his family was very strange, it was

beyond different.

While he may love them to death, each and every one but there were times where he often thought

Perhaps his mother had taken the wrong baby from the wrong crib at the hospital because as far as he was concerned, he saw himself as being the only sane person in the family!

He had two older brothers, Tommy and Jake, and both weren't that much different from each other.

Tommy was for ever living inside his fantasy world, wearing those ridiculous boxing gloves all day, everyday for as long as Chickery could remember and so it didn't come as any surprise that there were endless breakages around the home since Tommy would imagine himself as a famous boxer.

Personally, Chickery would be rather happy to have his weird brother strapped into a rocket ship and have the guy be shipped off to Mars, since the guy obviously did not belong to the real world, or else send him to a very good doctor!

Jake on the other hand, wasn't too bad but he wasn't exactly what some people may describe as "boyish" either.

He loved to dance, and would wear these odd beads and a flowing drape like the Africans made out of straws and he would dance like a boy possessed!

It wasn't surprising that since the whole family was weird, so too were his parents.

His mom Denise loved to dress up and would purchase expensive things and wear heavy make up and this went for her husband too, who loved to wear expensive brand clothing like Gucci, Prada, and Louis Vuitton

Chickery sighed to himself as he got up and left the bedroom.

Sooner or later his mom was going to come pounding on the bedroom door and announce her usual annoying declaration on 'what a beautiful, sunny day it is' and he wanted to avoid her chirpy tone at all cost.

He is not a morning person since he's always half awake and half in bed.

He couldn't get into the bathroom since the door was locked.

Great. There could only be one person in there at this time of hour in the morning and that was good old Tommy himself, probably talking up a storm inside that bathroom, drifting into his fantasy of being the world's most famous boxer and when he got lost in fantasy, he could be in there for hours talking to himself.

"Oh for goodness sake, you dreamy fool! Hurry up and get out already!" Chickery snapped.

There were mumbling from inside and then all were silent, and then out of nowhere there was a loud shattering sound, like the sound of a mirror being shattered! "Oh yesss, ladies and gentleman!" Tommy's voice rang out loud and clear.

The guy really was lost inside his universe at the moment!

"Everyone, I believe we have a winner!" This was followed by cheerful laughter and Chickery couldn't help himself but crack up laughing. There was no point in getting Tommy out of there, at least not now.

He broke only one mirror, and he may not get out until he wins another five gold medals for being the greatest boxer and that may cost up to another two broken windows being shattered.

Chickery went downstairs, still deciding on what he were to have for breakfast but he was startled when his mother came dancing out of nowhere at the bottom of the staircase.

She was twirling and dancing in delight, and she cracked up laughing.

Chickery stared at his mom in alarm and fear. "Err… mom? Are you ok today? What happened? Are you going somewhere?"

Denise kept on dancing and twirling around. "Everything's fine my dear, all is well."

Chickery was still staring wide eyed at his mom, unable to say another word.

Out of nowhere with out warning, loud music was blasting out from the living room and mother and Chickery cried out in shock.

Within seconds Denise's husband came dancing into the hallway only a foot away from the staircase and he was dressed up in the most lavish outfit ever, complete with sunglasses.

He was obviously dressing up like somebody from the 1970's, perhaps like a rock star.

Denise gasped, and then burst into giggles. Chickery blushed a deep red.

This was beginning to become too much for him to bare, he wanted to get away from this weird family of his before he too lost his own mind!

As he turned away and started walking off towards the kitchen there was a sound of shattered glass coming from upstairs.

"Yessss! Ladies and gentlemen, we again have a winner!" Tommy's cried out in victory.

Denise buried her face into her hands in frustration. "Oh, Tommy! Not again hun, I've just repaired that damn windows last week! Ahhhhrrrrrggggg!"

Chickery sighed and shook his head. Yes, everybody here was indeed beyond weird.

And frankly, he was very desperate to get out!

By the time Chickery and his two brothers stepped out onto the front porch of their home, Chickery felt relieved that they were able to get out at last after all of the commotion going on at the breakfast table.

Their school bus pulled up at the side of the curb as it always does.

Chickery and his brothers ran off down the sidewalk so they wouldn't miss it. Some of the neighborhood kids were also running down their driveways and were making their way to the curb, trying to catch the bus to school too.

Chickery felt their eyes focusing on him and he felt very uncomfortable.

These kids went to the same school as he and his brothers and they had also placed a label onto Chickery's family as a 'bunch of weirdo's.''

True, Chickery knew that his family was odd. He couldn't deny that, as much as he may want to. But Chickery wasn't in the mood to be teased about members of his own family.

He's had enough. He just hope the creeps would be quiet and leaves him alone. "Hey, weirdo!" one of the kids yelled out and the others cracked up laughing. "Weirdo! Weirdo! Weirdo!" They chanted together as they lined up at the bus stop. "Here comes the weirdo!"

Chickery felt his face growing red in embarrassment.

Ignoring the creeps, he got onto the bus and chose a seat that was far away from his brothers as possible, whom were both seated at the back.

The other kids went on the bus and found their own seats.

All of them had friends and none of them wanted to be seated anywhere near Chickery.

But they wouldn't stop staring at him, or his two brothers.

They all smirked and giggled. Chickery was used to their laughter and smirks but they were obviously pointing at something at the back of the bus.

Chickery slowly looked over his shoulders and he almost fainted. Jake was busy picking his nose and then he began smearing the sticky snots onto the window of the bus! Tommy as usual, was lost in his own fantasy world, thinking he was the world's greatest boxer.

He began punching the air with his boxing gloves and Jake was picking large globs of snot out of his nose.

Still punching the air, Tommy turned to the side and aimed his boxing gloves at the windows and it shattered!

Chickery was stunned as the bus driver came to a screeching stop and everybody covered their ears as a result of the dreadful noise.

With the windows of the bus now smashed to pieces, Tommy wore a big grin on his face.

He pumped the air in victory. "Everybody, I believe that we again have this year's greatest champion!"

The bus driver scowled angrily at Tommy. "And I believe your mother will be grounding you for the rest of your life once I send her the damn bill for the breakages you've caused on this bus! Now sit back and behave or else I'll really kick you out of the bus and you can walk to school!"

Chickery sunk deeper into his seat, his face flushed a deep red.

Everybody was now staring at him and his two brothers in silence but their smirks never went away.

Chickery wished the bus driver wouldn't look at Jake.

But no chance of that.

The bus driver spotted Jake wiping his sticky fingers onto the windows and then saw the snots dripping down the edges.

"You disgusting little brats!" The driver bellowed furiously. "That's it! I am not going to clean up that...that...disgusting mess of yours! No way will I pay for the broken window! Your mother will be getting a very expensive bill in the mail soon! Now get out of my bus! The driver pointed a finger at Chickery. "And yes, that goes for you too! You and your weird members of your family can get out of here!"

Chickery quickly got out while Jake and Tommy stomped out, pouting.

The bus started its engine again and slowly drove away.

The kids stuck their heads out of the windows and smirked.

"Weirdo's! You're all a bunch of weirdo's!"

Chickery and his brothers stood on the road and were covered in gas fumes as the bus disappeared down the road and out of sight.

Chickery threw his hands into the air. "Oh great! And so now what are we going to do?"

"What do you mean, what are we going to be doing?" Tommy snapped sarcastically. "What a stupid question to be asking! We'll just have to go to school ourselves."

"But we've just been kicked off the bus!" Chickery argued.

"Then we'll walk. Ever heard of walking, little brother?"

The three of them began walking ahead down the road but Chickery couldn't bring himself to stop complaining.

The hot sun was now shining very brightly in the sky and all three were sweating immensely. "I cannot believe that we're walking to school!" Chickery grumbled to himself.

"I most definitely cannot believe that we've got kicked off the bus! What were you thinking, Jake? Picking your nose? I mean...seriously!"

"Be quiet and just keep on walking!" Jake ordered softly, his face a deep red. "I have never felt so embarrassed in my life!" Chickery ranted again. Jake and Tommy came to a stop suddenly. "Oh, so we've embarrassed you, huh?" Jake asked snidely. "You bet you did!" Chickery retorted. "One of you broke a window and the other one picked his nose! I think that's enough for one day!"

"We didn't realize we were so embarrassing to be with!" Tommy snapped. "In that case we should go ahead and leave you behind."

Chickery crossed his arms. "I think that is the greatest thing I've heard all day." Jake and Tommy stomped off while Chickery wiped sweat off his face. "Hey! Wait up! Do you have anything to drink?"

Tommy turned around and sneered. "I have some juice in my bag. But I don't think you want to drink it...it may taste weird!"

The two brothers turned and walked off. Chickery sighed. Great. Now he was alone. But he sure wasn't going to school, not after what had happened!

So what was he going to do now?

Chickery paced the sidewalk for several minutes, feeling lost as to what he should do. He couldn't go back home since he didn't have a good excuse for not being at school and after that humiliating experience on the bus he was sure he'd be laughed at once he gets to school.

Chickery paced back and forth for awhile until the heat of the sun became too much for him to bare that he went over to a bus stop and sat down, deciding on where he was to go.

His mind was deep in thought and he drifted off into space until he spotted a large, colorful poster on the bulletin.

He realized that it was an advertisement for a brand new zoo called Arabia that had recently just opened up in town.

Feeling quite excited, he made up his own mind that he was going to attend the zoo in town and try and put this humiliating experience that just happened this morning behind him in the best way possible. There was, how ever, one tiny problem. The entry fee for the zoo was $6.50, and he had just enough for his bus fare.

But he was stubborn and he wanted desperately to go to the zoo, even if he had to stand outside and take a peek through the entrance gates, he'd still rather prefer to do that then go to school and have other kids laugh at him.

Feeling quite determined he boarded the bus as soon as it arrived at the curb.

Once inside, he felt guilty. He knew that he was going to get into so much trouble for not going to school but it wasn't his fault.

He was kicked off the bus and he was now the laughing stock of the town.

Feeling very satisfied, he broke out into a grin and started to relax as the bus drove off into town.

He had a good excuse now, but even he hoped that it was good enough of an excuse to bail him out of trouble.

The bus ride into town was a long one but since he'd never travelled into town on his own, he felt very excited.

Eventually, the excitement wore off and he found himself yawning and starting to fall asleep.

He had to pinch himself just to stay awake.

After what appeared to be an hour's journey into town, Chickery sat up with a jolt as he spotted the colorful letterings ahead that simply read: Arabia Zoo.

He was finally here!

He got off the bus and was awestruck by the scene that greeted him.

Adults of all ages, including small children were lined up outside the entrance to the zoo and the long line appeared to stretch on forever.

Everybody seemed to be quite excited, there were all smiles and laughter all around.

Chickery saw a big and very tall security officer standing by the entrance and was accepting golden tickets off each person before they were allowed to come inside the zoo.

Chickery stood on his tippy toes, hoping to score a better look on what the inside scenery was like, but the crowds were enormous and so he was very disappointed when he wasn't able to catch a glimpse of anything.

Dropping his gaze to the ground, he sulked off into the distance and slumped down onto a wooden bench and sat there gazing up at the tall entrance gates of the zoo.

"Hey, mate. No food is allowed into the area until you're done eating."

Chickery glared at the security officer who was talking to a very chubby kid, who was busy polishing off a melted chocolate bar.

The kid was grasping onto his entry ticket in one hand and there were melted chocolate dripping down the ticket.

The kid gave the security man a dirty look and stormed off to the side, ripping off his wrapper of the candy bar and for a moment he seemed to struggle keeping hold of his candy bar while he juggled with his sticky and gooey fingers off the ticket.

He was so busy and determined in eating his candy bar very quickly, probably so he could return to the long line and enter the zoo that he didn't see his chocolate covered ticket fall to the ground in the process.

Moments later Chickery joined the large crowd grasping onto the soiled ticket, his heart beating very hard.

He felt extremely nervous and he had to control his trembling fingers.

He gazed over at the chubby kid and saw that he was finishing his last bites of the candy bar.

The chubby kid then went on to lick his sticky fingers but a puzzled look came over him when he realized his ticket was gone.

"Hey, where did my ticket go?" He cried in shock.

He looked frantically around him but grew even more angry when he realized his ticket was nowhere in sight.

"Where is my ticket?" He yelled out angrily, his face beet red.

The large crowd turned to stare at him in silence.

The security man shook his head in disgust. "Silly little brat," he grumbled under his breath. "He brings food into the queue and now he lost the damn ticket!"

The crowd was now moving along much quicker and Chickery swallowed hard when he came up to the security man.

Slowly handing over the soiled ticket Chickery wished the security wouldn't get suspicious.

But the security stared at the dirty ticket for a moment and then glared at Chickery with suspicion evident in his eyes.

"I...umm...I...had some chocolate before my mom bought the ticket," Chickery fibbed, "I'm sorry about the mess. I hope it's still ok to go inside."

The security studied Chickery for a moment and then shook his head.

"You damn filthy kids. Seriously, first that guy over there and now you. Consider yourself lucky because I'm letting you in!"

Chickery burst out in a huge grin. "Thank you!"

Skipping inside, Chickery glared around at the awesome scenery that greeted his vision.

Animals of all walks of life were lined up in cages while some were moving around freely.

Chickery swallowed his guilt and tried to push it to the back of his mind.

Chickery stood among the large crowds inside the zoo and he wasn't able to budge since everywhere he turned he would be running into somebody, especially somebody's grandma.

People were pointing and talking and some had already taken out their cameras to take pictures.

Unable to control his excitement any longer, Chickery pushed his way through the crowds, upsetting several people but he didn't care.

He spotted one of his favorite animals, the colorful peacock bird with the colorful tail but while he studied it with fascination, the bird had a dark, stormy look on its face.

Several people cooed over the bird, some began snapping pictures and this appeared to upset the peacock even more.

Chickery wondered over to the bird, wanting a better look at it upon closer inspection.

"Hey! I was here first!" A young kid cried out angrily," go away! This is my spot!"

Chickery flashed the kid a dirty look. "You don't own this zoo and so why don't you go away?"

The boy looked shocked and he then ran off into the crowds.

"Nice move there," the peacock commented, "I was dying for that kid to go away. He was starting to annoy me!"

Chickery gasped in shock. "You can talk? Wow, that's awesome!"

The peacock frowned. "What's that supposed to mean? Of course I can talk! I see your mouth is moving and so obviously you can talk yourself!"

"What's wrong with you?" Chickery asked. "Why are you so mean to me?"

The peacock rolled its eyes. "You try spending two days with-out food and see how you feel. You would feel quite unhappy yourself!"

Several more people snapped pictures at the bird and it frowned deeply as it bustled around in annoyance. "I hope these creeps would quit it with the cameras! Damn fools!"

Chickery was intrigued. "Why aren't you being fed?"

"For someone so little, you sure ask a lot of questions!" The peacock snapped in irritation. "Because

There isn't a responsible creep here who cares about us, that's why! Look around you, at the many others whom I call my family—you'll see that they too are miserable."

Chickery glared around at the animals nearby from the koalas, to the giraffes and realized that they both appeared pale, just like the peacock itself.

"That's very sad to hear," Chickery muttered, "my parents would never let me go hungry. They take very good care of me...even though they're very weird."

"Awww, isn't that a clever, pretty fairy tale?" The peacock said sarcastically. "And so why don't you go off and live happily ever after then, hmmm?"

Chickery gave the bird a nasty look and stomped off, he's fed up with the bird's rudeness.

He walked around the entire place, gazing from one animal to the next and when he spotted a lion nearby he stopped dead in his tracks.

Chickery wanted to go and say hello but he was terrified.

He'd been told that lions can be very dangerous when they want to be and he wasn't sure saying hello was such a good idea.

As if reading his thoughts, an elephant suddenly trumpeted its trunk, startling everybody in the process. Some even yelled out in fright.

"Don't even think about going near that creep," the elephant declared.

"He isn't going to talk to you. He's very odd. He never talks to anyone around here. I personally, think he's very weird."

Chickery took a deep breath and tried to calm down.

The lion was weird? He could understand that since his own family was very weird!

Chickery gave the elephant a grateful smile. "Thanks for the advice, but I think I'm going to say hello anyways." The elephant shrugged. "Fine with me. But don't say I didn't warn you."

Chickery walked slowly up to the lion, who was lying down glaring at everybody around him with suspicious eyes.

The lion noticed the unexpected guest standing before him and he grumbled slightly, his eyes wide and flashing a terrifying red.

The lion rose from its sitting position and gazed expectedly at Chickery. Chickery swallowed hard, regretting that perhaps he'd made a mistake.

"What do you want?" The lion demanded.

"N...n...nothing. I err...I just wanted to say hi...," Chickery stuttered, feeling frustrated.

The lion appeared surprised. "You wanted to say hi? What's your reason for coming over   here? What do y   do you really want?" Chickery frowned at the lion's rude nature.

His questions were becoming ridiculous. "As I've said, I just wanted to say hi. I thought we could be friends, that is if you want to."

The lion smirked. "You want something, I know you do. Don't treat me like a fool.

I know people like you are always seeking something! So, I'll say it one last time. What do you want?" Chickery's fear slowly faded away and he started feeling very angry.

"What's wrong with you?" Chickery snapped, his face flushing a deep red. "I've never met somebody so obnoxious in my life! You're so paranoid!"

The lion's eyes flashed red and widened. "Don't tell me what I am, you little twerp! If you aren't going to tell me on what you want, then get out of here!"

"Fine! I'll do just that!" Chickery yelled back and began to stomp off but then a thought came to him and a smirk grew on his face.

He turned around and faced the lion. "You really are a big weirdo. I have to agree with the elephant. He was right about you. I think you're one lonely weirdo who never talks to anyone around here."

The lion snarled at him threateningly. "You're beginning to get on my nerves, keep this up and I'll eat you."

"Oh, you won't do that," Chickery chuckled. "If you eat me then who will be your friend? You don't talk to anybody here!"

"What makes you think I want to be your friend?" The lion demanded.

"Well, I'm talking to you and so far am the only one who is doing so. Nobody else will. They think you're too weird."

Chickery smiled and extended his hand. "So what do you say? You want to be my friend?"

The lion glared at Chickery for a moment in silence.

He turned away abruptly, his expression stern. "Go away. I'm not interested in being your friend. You're lying, I know it. I won't play the fool. You cannot fool me!"

"I am not lying to you!" Chickery exclaimed frustratedly. "Gosh, all I want is to be your friend that is all. What makes you think I'm lying?" "People always lie to me," the lion snapped. "They had tried to trick me several times before. I am a lion. I am smart and I'm no fool!" Chickery immediately felt great sympathy for his new friend. "Yes, you are a smart lion. A very brave and strong lion. But don't let those people bother you, ok? They are mean people, they aren't nice. But I'm a good person and I like you and I want us to be friends. I will never lie or try to trick you, I promise!"

The lion stayed silent for a moment and then sighed. "Alright. I will trust you. But don't ever try to play me for a fool or else I will eat you immediately!"

Chickery smiled gleefully. "It's a deal! It's good to have a new friend at last. By the way, my name's Chickery."

The lion smiled. "Nice to have you as a friend, Chickery."

"So what's your name?" Chikery asked.

The lion's smile vanished immediately and he didn't respond for a long time. "It's...Larry. My name is Larry."

"I'm so happy to have you as my friend, Larry," Chickery declared.

He felt so overwhelmed with excitement that he couldn't stand still.

How ever, as happy as he was, there was just one small problem.

He had to go home soon. He was going to be in so much trouble if he didn't go home.

His parents would be very worried.

"Listen, Larry...I'm happy to be friends with you but I have to go now. I'm so sorry," Chickery rambled on quickly.

Larry's smile vanished and his face grew dark red in anger.

"I knew it! You've tricked me! You're going to pay for this! You'll be so damn sorry!"

The lion leaped up into the air and roared at the top of its lungs!

Chickery staggered backwards and screamed in fright as the lion started leaping at him! Chickery screamed and turned to run while the crowd grew scared and every body began to run away. Immediately five men jumped onto the lion and got hold of him. The crowd slowly ran out of the entrance gates but chickery stopped running and turned around to take a look at the commotion.

BY now the men had gotten hold of the lion and were dragging him into an empty cage. The lion roared fiercely but one of the men slammed the cage door shut and padlocked it. chickery's eyes watered and he swallowed hard. The lion threw itself against the cage and the steel door rattled loudly. "You creep!" The lion cried out angrily. "I'm going to eat you somehow! Just wait and see!"

Chikery's body trembled and he turned around to run out of the entrance gates. Later that night, the owner of the zoo paced restlessly outside the lion's cage.

The man shook his head in disgust. "You stupid, troublemaker of an animal! Did You realize how much trouble you've caused to this zoo today? Do you? You've sacred all of my customers away and thanks to you, these people will never come back because this place had become too dangerous! They are too scared to return here! Stupid fool! You will be punished!"

The man threw his half eaten apple he'd been holding in his hand and it landed onto the lion's head. The lion roared aggressively in defense. "That's what you get for ruining my business today?" The man declared triumphantly.

"I will get rid of you tonight myself, but I'll have my dinner first. Then I'll be back for you!"

The man turned and stormed off into his office while the lion leaped against the cage. Once inside his office, the man took down one of his rifles down from the wall where he held many of his collections and from there he loaded the rifle with bullets.

Grinning with satisfaction, he calmly reached out for a greasy but crispy piece of bacon strip off his dinner plate and devoured it greedily.

He was so lost in his own pleasure that he didn't notice the dark shadow sauntering into the room.

As he reached for another piece of bacon, the large, dark figure leaped into the air and attacked him!

Chickery got off the bus the next day and there he would stand outside the front entrance gates, just as he had done the previous day, gazing up at the colorful letterings above the gates.

He wasn't supposed to be here since he was in big trouble over not going to school yesterday and he'd been punished enough by being sent off to his room with out being given dinner.

But he couldn't stay away from the zoo, not after what had happened yesterday. There were too many unresolved business going on that had to be solved right away.

"Larry" himself had thought that Chickery tried to trick him, to make a fool out of him and he wanted to come back and correct the misunderstanding.

He wanted to be friends with Larry, if only Larry himself would give him another chance.

Chickery noticed something strange at the zoo that day—there wasn't a single soul lining outside the gates but as he got closer he realized in surprise that the zoo was closed.

Peering through the padlocked gates Chickery could see the paramedic's vehicle parked inside and he spotted one of the workers load a stretcher into the vehicle.

Something was terribly wrong. Something must've happened yesterday after he'd left the zoo.

Chickery felt a cold chill race down his spine.

But what had happened exactly?

Chickery's mind was racing with various thoughts on what he believed may had happened inside the zoo yesterday.

But it was pointless since he was never going to find out the truth.

With a heavy heart, Chikery walked off down the street.

He couldn't stop thinking about Larry, especially on how angry Larry had been yesterday! He could only hope that Larry was ok and that Larry would forgive him.

Chickery really wanted to be friends with Larry.

Realizing that he had nowhere to go for several hours he wondered over to the park and sat down under a tree, watching other people play and enjoying themselves.

Chikery felt for ever depressed as he sat there under the cool shades of the big tree and he couldn't stop thinking about Larry. As he drifted into his own thoughts, he didn't hear the sound of cracked dry leaves from behind him.

The large dark figure loomed closer towards Chickery but the guy still had no clue that he had a stranger seated near him.

The stranger was breathing heavily and Chickery was startled out of his own deep thoughts.

His eyes widened in alarm, Chickery spun around and breathed in relief when he realized that it was only Larry but his presence made Chickery very nervous.

He knew that Larry was still very angry at him.

"Gosh, you almost scared me to death!" Chickery exclaimed, trying to calm himself down.

Larry smirked. "Too bad you didn't because after that trick you've pulled, I wasn't too happy with you."

"Yes, about that," Chickery interrupted, "I wanted to let you know that you've misunderstood my intentions. I wasn't trying to trick you into anything but I had to go home or else my folks would get mad. I'm not playing games. I just want us to be friends." Larry sat quietly while he absorbed the information he'd been told. "Really? So you weren't trying to pull anything?" Larry asked hesitantly. "I just want to be your friend," Chickery said, "that is, if you still want to."

Larry stayed silent while he gazed at Chickery, a look of uncertainty darkened his features.

"How can I trust you, though? I don't even know you!"

"Well, I'm not a stranger anymore. You've met me yesterday and so let us be friends ok?"

Chickery pleaded sincerely, "let me show you that I'm a good person and that I can be a good friend, too."

Larry remained unconvinced. "O don't let know about this. I still think you're up to something and I refuse to be the fool! I just won't!" Chickery sighed in frustration. "Quit being so paranoid and let me be your friend ok? I know that you're lonely and that is ok because I am lonely too. But we can help each other out by being friends-that way we won't be lonely anymore!"

Chickery waited for Larry's response but when Larry remained silent Chickery knew that he had to try harder. "Listen, I know that you're lonely and so don't lie to me! I know that deep down you need and want a friend, just like everyone else. So why are you being so difficult? I want us to be friends!"

"I have my own reason for being the way I am," Larry snapped, his eyes flashed red again. "Well, what ever the reason is, I am here to help you," Chickery explained patiently. "Do you really want to be alone all the time? Surely you feel lonely and sad too." Larry shrugged. "Im used to it. I've been alone for years now."

"But you don't have to be alone for ever, I am here for you," Chickery pressed on. "Come on, let's be friends. I know you'll be glad to have me as a friend!" "Don't try to be smart," Larry warned, "You don't know me, remember?" "Well, I know your name," Chickery said grinning. "So, Larry. Do you like chocolate fudge ice cream? I'm in the mood for something cold!" "I love chocolate fudge," Larry exclaimed, his face brightened up immediately. "Great, then! I know of an excellent ice cream parlor in town, so let's go?" The two of them held each other's hands and skipped into town. People in the streets gasped and screamed at the sight of Larry while car horns honked but the two friends ignored the noise and entered Gianni's Kingdom of Ice cream. Chickery ordered a large bowel of chocolate fudge for the two of them and they both sat down at a table to share the ice cream together. People inside the parlor turned to stare and some whispered and gasped. Chickery watched on in shock as Larry took the bowel and gobbled the ice cream within seconds and then he burped out loud.

Chickery felt very angry and shocked. He hasn't had a taste of the damn fudge and already the bowel was empty! But he didn't want to ruin their friendship by getting into a silly fight over ice cream.

"Can I have some more?" Larry asked. "I'm still hungry! Let's have some more ice cream!" Chickery stormed off to pay for another bowel but he wasn't happy with his new friendship with Larry! Chickery returned to their table with a huge bowel of ice cream but before he could sit down Larry snatched the bowel and gobbled it down! Chickery felt speechless. He wanted so badly to be friends with Larry, but he was beginning to feel like he'd made a mistake. So far their friendship had a problem but Larry's too busy licking the bowel to notice. Chickery breathed deeply and tried not to get upset over the ice cream.

There was something that bothered him very much. "How did you escape from the zoo?" Chickery asked. Larry looked up from the bowel and shrugged. "I had to leave the zoo because I didn't like it there. I was always alone. Besides, the people there aren't nice to me." Chickery nodded slowly. "No, I suppose they aren't so nice over there at the zoo." Larry went on to lick the bowel clean. "I'm glad you wanted to be friends. I'm having a very good time." Chickery forced a smile onto his face. "Yes, me too," he lied.

Too bad I can't say the same for myself, he thought to himself.

Larry wiped his mouth and gave out another loud burp.

Chickery frowned at his friend's rude nature but was startled when he heard a man's voice yelling out, "Help me! Help me!"

Larry's stomach growled and then it went on growling for several seconds.

Oddly enough, the voice seemed to be coming from inside Larry's stomach!

"Did you hear that?" Chickery gasped, "I think I've heard something."

"I didn't hear anything," Larry replied, staring uncomfortably at the table.

"So, let's go back to your place. I'm a little tired, I need some rest."

"My place?" Chickery asked, his mouth wide opened. "But don't you have a place of your own?"

"Where will I go?" Larry snapped. "I'm not returning to the zoo, ok? Besides, you said that you're my friend and that you'd help me?"

"I am your friend. I don't think my parents would be ok with this ," Chickery stuttered.

"Fine, forget it," Larry snapped. "I'm a fool to believe that you're my friend. You aren't a friend at all! You are not helping me in finding a place to stay!"

"Ok! Alright, fine!" Chickery yelled out. "You can stay at my place. For tonight. Only."

Larry smiled widely but Chickery rolled his eyes. So far this friendship was beginning to feel like a massive mistake!

The bus ride home was a nightmare for Chickery.

He was in a bad mood thanks to Larry's selfish nature and rudeness back at the ice cream parlor but once they're inside the bus, Larry became a nightmare to deal with.

Larry immediately lay down on the bus seat like it was his own bed but the bus driver hadn't said a damn thing, probably felt too sacred to speak out!

The bus was very crowded and there aren't enough seats and so Chickery had to stand through out the ride home.

He hated to admit it but Larry's obnoxious behavior reminded Chickery of his own brothers! His own family was weird enough as it was with out him having to deal with another oddball!

Suddenly there was a disgusting, foul stench drifting in the air and Chickery grew pale.

People were coughing and turning around to stare at him angrily.

Larry laughed outrageously while Chickery's face blushed a deep red. Denise nearly collapsed in shock to the patio floor when she answered the door and saw a large monster standing before her!

Larry rudely went inside and explored the house, shocking poor Richard who entered the kitchen.

Larry raided the fridge and cabinets for a moment before slumping down onto the sofa and watched Tv.

Denise and Richard pulled Chickery into the kitchen. "What on earth is going on here? Who is that? What's he doing here?"

Chickery sighed. "Trust me, it's a long story. But relax, he's only staying here for tonight only."

Denise gasped. "What? For tonight? But why?"

"I'll explain everything later on mom, I'm just too tired right now!" Chickery exclaimed.

Hours later the family got into the messy kitchen to prepare dinner together. They opened the fridge and cabinets and realized in shock that it was all empty!

"Hey! Where's all of the food gone off to?" Tommy cried.

Larry appeared suddenly at the doorway with a stupid grin on his face. "I'm starving! So, what's for dinner?"

Chickery's face grew stormy like a thunder cloud.

Hours later Chickery and his family watched Larry in astonishment as he wolfed down the entire Larry batch of pancakes Denise had cooked up for him.

Larry burped out loud and he still wore that annoying, stupid grin. "Have you got any pizzas?"

Chickery couldn't control his anger anymore. "I think you've eaten more than enough! Meanwhile, my family and I are dying of hunger!"

Larry shrugged carelessly. "Well, I was hungry. Besides, your mom cooked the pancakes for me."

"She did not! She cooked those for our family! You're just a house guest!" Larry's face darkened dangerously. "You took me home into your house! You have to feed me, you can't just let me starve! I am your friend! Remember?" Chickery crossed his arms. "Don't remind me. I'm beginning to think it was a mistake!"

Larry gazed in silence at Chickery, a look of shock on his face.

He then opened up his mouth and roared at the top of his lungs and leaped into the air. Everybody screamed and jumped back in fright.

The entire house appeared to have shook wildly, even the floors felt like it was vibrating!

Denise immediately took action. "Calm down, Larry. It's ok, don't get upset. I'll make you some of my most delicious pizzas, how does that sound?" Larry gave another loud roar but his angry features softened and he eventually settled down. "Fine, make me your finest pizzas! I am still very hungry!"

Denise immediately sprung into action and started preparing her ingredients.

Two hours later she collapsed into a chair after baking twenty pizzas.

Larry on the other hand started digging into the pile of pizzas.

Chickery was beyond disgusted at the sight of Larry and so he stormed upstairs.

Denise turned to her husband and said," I think we have a problem here. Our son Chickery needs a new friend and this person here is not acceptable!" "What do you have in mind?" Richard asked.

"He needs a more sensible, reliable friend," Denise said. "Like a cat." "A cat?" Richard asked, astonished

"Yes, a cat is a great choice," Denise declared, "I cannot think of anyone else more suitable than a cat."

"But honey, isn't all this a bit sudden?" Richard asked. "Seriously, a cat?"

"Our son must be lonely," Denise said, "I think that's why he brought this lousy fool into our home! I can't stand the sight of him! I'm glad he's only staying for tonight though!"

"Yes, I'm glad too," Richard grumbled.

Meanwhile, Larry had wolfed down more than half the pile of pizzas.

But he'd overheard the conversation that Denise had with her husband and now he turned to glare at the, his eyes flashing red with fury. The couple didn't seem to notice him glaring at them, since they were still talking to each other.

Larry sneered and in one firm grip he munched down the pile of pizzas and went upstairs to Chickery's room.

Chikery groaned at the sight of Larry wondering into his room.

He turned over in bed and pulled the blankets to his shoulders.

"Hope you've enjoyed my mom's cooking, because once tonight is over you're leaving this house!" There was a long period of silence. "I thought I was your friend," Larry said, his voice surprisingly soft and tender. He sounded hurt. "Well, that was a mistake. I thought you were a good person, but you're not," Chickery snapped. "You're too damn selfish! I don't like you anymore, ok? You're leaving tomorrow."

"Listen, I'm sorry for everything's that's happened tonight," Larry said, "don't be mad at me." "I'm tired Larry, don't want to talk anymore tonight." "But I am very sorry! What more can I say? I'm so sorry," Larry cried. "We can talk more about what to do with our friendship tomorrow," Chickery snapped. With out needing an invitation, Larry climbed into bed with Chickery but due to his size he succeeded in knocking poor Chickery out onto the floor!

BLUE
HAPPY
MAD
SAD
PEEVED
CONFUSED
IRRITATED
LOVE
GROSS
DISGUSTED
BRIGHT
SILLY
FOOLISH
DUMB
TALKATIVE
HATE
DISLIKE
JELLY
SPARKLING
SNORTING
FLYING
RIPPING
CREAMY

chickery remained on the floor in shock. Larry burst out laughing. "oops. sorry about that. I guess I'm too big to fit into this bed."

chikery felt his whole body growing hot in anger. "oh jeez. No worries. You can sleep in my bed tonight. After all, You'll be out of here by tomorrow."

Larry rolled over to his side and pulled the blanket over his shoulders, a smirk spreading over his face. "we'll see about that," he muttered softly to himself before closing his eyes.

The next morning chickery woke up and was surprised to find that his own bed was empty, and he wondered what had happened to Larry. But he knew deep down that he felt very relieved and was happy to have life going back to normal as it was before, and sad as it was, he didn't really care on what happened or where Larry was at the moment. Shrugging his shoulders, he got up and went downstairs to get some breakfast before going to school. unfortunately, his new found happiness was crushed to pieces when he spotted Larry seated at the breakfast table with his family in the kitchen. "Good morning!" Larry greeted cheerfully. "come have some bagels. I bought them this morning and it's still warm! come have some!" "You bought the bagels?" chickery asked in disbelief. "But why? what are You up to now?" Larry looked hurt. "can't I be nice? I wanted to do something nice to thank You for being my friend. And for letting me stay." "well, as nice as all this is," chickery sighed and sat down at the table, "You're still leaving after breakfast." Larry's smile vanished. "B...b...but...but...I am Your friend! I don't have anybody! Nobody likes me!" Larry covered his face and to everybody's surprise he began to cry hysterically.

chickery felt very bad and his sympathy went out to Larry. "oh, alright! You can stay! But not too long though! I'll find You another place to stay later on!"

Larry stopped crying and broke out in a big grin. "I'll wait for You to come home so we can play together, just like good friends should." chikery rolled his eyes and began to eat. when he boarded the bus, Larry waved excitedly. "BYe, BYe! See You later this afternoon!" chickery ignored him and the bus droved off.

Later that day in school, chikery went to the library to collect some newspaper articles for his assignment. He got large stacks of old newspapers and started looking through the oldest ones. He came across a large picture in a newspaper and froze in his tracks.

Something was wrong here...

Chickery couldn't believe what he was seeing. He was hoping that his eyes were playing tricks onto him but the evidence was right there in the newspaper!

What on earth was Larry doing being featuring on the newspaper's front cover? Chickery thought to himself in confusion.

Since when did he become famous? What exactly did he do to become famous? Why is he there?

Chickery shook his head. No, perhaps he's imagining things. He had to be. Maybe this picture of the lion isn't Larry. It had to be someone else!

There are plenty of lions out there that looked similar to each other!

Chickery read the newspaper and sighed in relief when he realized that the lion in the picture wasn't Larry.

It was another lion, who went by the name of "Liaises", and the story itself in the newspaper was quite scary.

Apparently this aggressive lion that went by the name of Liaises had attacked several of the residents in town and most of them were either killed instantly or badly injured.

Liaises possessed a very bad temper, the newspaper stated in the article.

In fact, this lion had a dangerous anger in which Liaises himself wasn't able to control and what was shocking was that despite the many savage attacks he's made on the residents of the town, it wasn't the first time he'd done it. As Chickery quickly leafed through the pole of newspapers, he realized that at least ten newspapers had been dedicated on Liaises, and on the horrible things in which he'd done to the people of the town.

But as Chikery read on in fascination, he came across an article about the lion running away from home and lived a very quiet life out in the wild and how he was later captured and being brought over to Arabia Zoo.

Chikery felt his mind spinning as he noticed the odd coincidence in the story.

A lion living out there in the wild? And being captured and bought over to Arabia Zoo? He felt a cold icy chill race down his spine as the realization came down on him hard.

He felt very scared and pushed the pile of newspapers away and ran out of the library. His family could be in great danger at this very moment and he had to save them!

WEL
WELCOME

He had to get rid of Liaises right away before he killed anybody!

Moments later Chikery was seated on the bus. He was leaving school and is trying to hurry on home.

His family must be in grave danger and he simply had to save them!

Chickery still couldn't believe that he'd been such a fool in believing that Larry was a good person and that he would make a good friend!

Chickery felt like he was the one who had been fooled and in a way he had been. Larry was a liar that much was for sure. No doubt about it.

He had used and lied to Chickery from the beginning and Chickery wanted to get Larry out of his life starting from today!

Chickery hugged himself tightly since he was shaking with anger.

The bus came to a stop at the curbside and he got out and ran all the way home. Not surprisingly, he found Larry lying on the sofa, watching TV. Larry broke out in a wide grin. "Oh, well! Well! Well! Isn't this a surprise?"

Chickery smirked. "It wont be a surprise for much longer Liaises!"

Larry froze. "What? Who's Liaises? What are you talking about?"

"Oh, quit lying to me, ok? I know the truth now!" Chickery yelled, "You're such a liar! A liar and a dangerous creep! I want you out! Get out of my house!" Larry's face grew a dangerous shade of red. "How did you find out about me?" "Does it matter?" Chickery snapped. "You're a liar and dangerous! I don't want to be your friend anymore! We aren't friends anymore so get out!" Larry burst into tears. "Why are you doing this to me? Why are you being so mean?" Chickery pushed him roughly. "I said get out! Leave! Now!"

Larry cried hysterically. "I know that you don't mean it! I will go now, give you some time to calm down. I shall come back later on."

Chickery opened the front door. "Don't bother doing that! I want you out of here! Out!" Larry stormed out the door and Chikery slammed it shut.

Feeling exhausted and upset, he went into the guest room and lay down on the sofa. Moments later the door swung opened and he sat up in alarm. He was afraid that Larry had come back and that he himself was walking through that door right now!

But to his relief, his parents came bouncing inside. "We're home! We're home!" Denise sang out cheerfully.

She and Richard were holding onto a large box, covered in a red cloth. "We have a surprise for you!"

HELLO
DON'T
TALK

Chikery raised his eyebrows questioningly. "Uh oh. I don't think I like the sound of this. More surprises? I think I've had my own special surprises today."

Denise frowned. "What surprises have you had? Don't tell me that creep Larry did something in this house! I knew he must've done something! I knew it! Why did you let him stay in our house again?"

Chickery slumped down onto the sofa lounge. "Because I've been a fool, that's why. But...anyways. We don't have to worry about him anymore. He's gone."

"Gone? What do you mean he's gone?" Denise asked, "What happened?" Chickery shrugged. "Simple really. I kicked him out. It's a shame I didn't do it earlier!"

"Oh, I'm so glad he's gone," Richard exclaimed. "Good on you, son."

"So, what's with the box?" Chickery asked, he was desperate to change the subject.

As far as he' concerned, Larry was gone and it's time to move on.

Denise broke out into a smile. "Well, honey. We just thought maybe you've been feeling lonely lately. Perhaps all you need is a friend." "Yes, I do need a friend...a good one," Chickery admitted, "I just hope who-ever it is would be honest."

"Oh, you're going to love your new friend," Denise gushed. "You're going to love him!" "Him?" Chickery asked, looking confused.

Denise took off the red cloth and inside the box was an adorable plump kitten. "Honey, meet Wilbert. I bought him for you! I hope he'll be a good friend to you."

Chickery gazed at the adorable kitten and broke out laughing. "Ohhhh, he's so beautiful. Thanks, mom!"

He got Wilbert out of the box and cuddled him.

Wilbert purred in contentment while Denise and Richard beamed in happiness.

Outside the living room window Larry was spying on the family.

His eyes flashed a deep red and he snarled at the sight of Chickery cuddling the kitten.

M
1 2 3
4 5 6

Larry pounded his fists against the brick wall as he observed how happy Chickery was.

He felt a sharp stab of jealousy. He wished he was the one being cuddled and being shown affection-problem was, it wasn't him. Never had been. Larry himself had never felt like he'd received proper love or affection from anybody. Especially from his own family. Larry breathed heavily, trying his best to calm down but all he felt was this incredible rage. He really felt angry at Chickery that moment. Larry himself was used to being alone. He was used to living a quiet life. He didn't enjoy it, but he accepted the fact that everybody thought and saw him as a weirdo. Maybe that's why nobody wanted to be his friend and he even accepted that, too. He was so used to being alone until Chikery came along and wanted to be his friend and he had fought the temptation. He really did try, but in the end his loneliness won and he was intrigued in giving this a try. The last two days had been the best in Larry's miserable, lonely life.

For once, he had a friend-someone who he could talk to. It both felt strange since he'd never trusted or let anyone into his life, but at the same time he couldn't deny that it was a nice change. He hated to admit it to himself, but for once he actually felt happy! But now he was back to square one, right back to the very beginning where he is alone.

Again. He expected himself to be used to feeling lonely, to accept it quickly and move on, but somehow he couldn't.

He simply couldn't handle it. He couldn't stand the silence anymore because it drove him crazy. He didn't want to go back to being alone anymore. He wanted a friend in his life.

But he'd lost Chickery as a friend today and Larry felt this feeling of great emptiness. He felt so alone.

He wished desperately that Chickery had simply left him alone in the first place! Glaring with hate in his eyes, Larry took one last look at the happy family and then disappeared from sight after that. If Chickery thought that he'd gotten rid of Larry that easily, he was very wrong! Later that evening, Denise and her husband walked out onto their patio after dinner and they hugged each other on their success in making their son so happy.

They kissed and while they were lost in their own bliss, a large shadow swept over them.

Chikcery gasped when he heard the sound of shrieking coming from the front porch. He on the hand was seated in the guest room's floor, engaging in some fun building a house using wooden blocks but now the fun was interrupted. Chikcery turned to wilbert, who was glaring out at the window. "what on earth is that noise?" Chikcery asked, his voice shaking in fear. wilbert stared back at Chickery with large glassy eyes and said nothing. Chickery got up and raced to the front door, opening it hastily and peeked out. Chikcery felt a cold chill race down his spine. He was now scared and was very worried about his parents, who seemed to disappear into thin air. Did they decide to go somewhere at the last minute? Chickery suspected that Larry had something to do with this and he shivered at the thought. He glared up at the cloudy, night sky and was surprised to find rain drips falling down. It started to drizzle at first but quickly poured down hard. Chickery turned to go back inside but paused when he spotted a dark figure in the driveway. It was Larry, glaring back at him with sad tearful eyes. "what are You still doing here?" Chikcery snapped. "Please, go away! Stay away from my house!" "Don't push me away," Larry pleaded. "Please let me come in. It's raining. I'm so cold! Plus, I have nowhere to go!" Chickery hesitated

by the doorway for a long moment but he felt great sympathy for Larry who was cold, soaked and shaking. He opened the door wide opened and Larry quickly rushed inside. Chickery hoped desperately that he hasn't made another big mistake. Larry wondered around the hallway but came to a stop outside the guest room where wilbert was seated on the floor. Chikery saw Larry's eyes widened in anger and flashing its usual red color. He heard wilbert screeching from the guest room and he shut the front door. "I'll go get You a towel, You're dripping all over the floor," Chickery said grimly. "But please know this: You're only staying here until the rain stops. After that You'll be leaving. Is that understood?" Larry nodded and then fell silent. "I appreciate You letting me in like this, You're a good person Chickery," Larry said, "a very good friend indeed." Chikery didn't reply, he turned to go upstairs to find a spare towel and he returned moments later. while Larry dried himself off with the towel, Chickery went into the guest room and tried to look for wilbert. He found wilbert hiding behind a sofa and he carried him out into the hallway. "It's ok, wilbert," Chickery cooed at his new friend, "I know You're scared of the lightning but I am here." Chikery smirked when he spotted Larry glaring at him as he cuddled wilbert in his arms. "oops, I forgot to introduce my new friend to You...Larry." Bringing wilbert closer, Chikery gazed lovingly at his adorable kitten. "Larry, meet wilbert. Isn't he just the greatest? He's my new friend!" Larry looked hurt and was quiet for several seconds. "Nice to meet You, wilbert," he said finally, his face surprisingly friendly and gentle as he touched little wilbert. The kitten meowed loudly and sunk deeper into Chikery's arms. "oh, I guess he doesn't like You," Chickery said sarcastically. "Little wilbert is very clever. He recognizes liars when he meets one." "oh, he'll like me soon," Larry replied confidently. Smiling, he added, "once he gets to know me better."

Chickery frowned at Larry's unusual friendly behavior.

Larry was behaving very odd at the moment and Chikery couldn't understand on what caused him to change.

But Chikery was tired when it came to Larry because he found the lion to be very unpredictable.

It was like Larry had two different people living inside of him: he could be nice and friendly but very obnoxious the next minute.

Chikery couldn't care less about Larry since they weren't friends anymore.

But he is very angry at Larry for being a liar from the beginning and if there's anything Chikery hated the most, it is liars!

"I love Wilbert so much," Chikery gushed, patting and kissing his kitten while observing Larry's reaction.

Larry was quiet but eventually smiled. "I'm happy for you. I can see that this kitten makes you very happy."

"Oh, he does. He sure does," Chikcery exclaimed, laughing. "He makes me so happy. He's so perfect. So...honest."

"Who're you talking to?" Tommy asked from his bedroom doorway. When he got downstairs he stopped. "Oh, I see somebody is back."

Larry stood very awkwardly in the hallway while Chikery smirked.

"What is he doing back here?" Tommy demanded. "Didn't you kick him out hours ago?"

"Oh, he's only staying here while the rain stops," Chikery said with fake sweetness.

He opened the front door and peered outside.

"The rain had stopped. I think you better leave," he said to the lion.

Larry nodded sadly and returned the towel. "Thanks for letting me stay." With-out another word, he wondered outside and disappeared into the darkness.

"What a weirdo," Tommy remarked, shaking his head.

Chickery gazed into the darkness outside, but he felt very troubled. Something just doesn't feel right. "Yes, he sure is weird," Chickery agreed, closing the front door.

Chikery wondered back into the living room to play the wooden blocks, carrying adorable Wilbert with him.

Tommy followed his brother into the guest room. "Man, that guy sure is weird. I hope he never comes back here. He's caused enough problems." "Yeah, tell me about it," Chickery muttered under his breath. "But let's not talk about him anymore ok? He's gone already."

"He was strange, though," Tommy ranted again. "I was expecting for him to go mad like he used to be before but he's so…I don't know… so…nice. Isn't that odd?"

Chickery didn't respond. Deep down he couldn't stop thinking about Larry's sudden change in attitude.

He wondered whether Larry himself may be up to something but when Wilbert meowed at him, he decided that he no longer cared.

Larry was gone for-ever and he wasn't a concern for Chickery anymore.

Chickery patted and kissed the affectionate Wilbert. "Where is Jake?" He asked, desperate to change the subject immediately.

Tommy shrugged. "Up in his room, I guess."

He kneeled down onto the floor to play with his brother and Wilbert.

Meanwhile, unbeknownst to them, a dark shadow was moving around outside. The rain had returned and in its place came the loud crackling of thunder.

The dark figure leaped onto the side walls of the house and crawled up, its breath heavy and raspy as it neared the top bedroom windows which had the lights turned on.

Inside that room, Jake was seated on the floor, caught up with his video games, gazing at the TV screen across the room.

He was so caught up in playing his video games that he didn't notice the large hand on his window sill.

The large hand reached for the latch on the window and slowly it was pulled back, letting in a blast of cold air.

Jake shivered in the cold breeze but kept on playing.

He suddenly gasped when he felt something wet and hairy touch the back of his neck.

Turning around, his eyes widened and he screamed in terror.

Chikery and Tommy heard the loud screams from upstairs and they both gasped in surprise.

They glared at each other wide eyed.

"What was that?" Tommy whispered, his face going pale.

Poor Wilbert grew terrified and screeched as he ran across the room and hid under the table.

Chikery stayed silent, hoping for some kind of sign as to what had happened. "I...I...wouldn't have the slightest clue. But that was a scream, I'm sure it is." "It's probably Jake," Tommy commented, "he's playing video games and must've lost several times and is now getting upset over his low score." "I don't know," Chickery muttered, "I think there is more to it than that."

Chickery frowned as he observed Tommy's face. "What's wrong with you?" Tommy's face was pale and he was shaking like a leaf.

"Tommy? Tommy? Will you please answer me? You're starting to scare me!" Chickery exclaimed. "Did you see that?" Tommy whispered, pointing at the window.

"Did I see what?" Chickery asked, feeling more confused than ever.

"Something is outside our house! I saw somebody running past our window!"

Tommy yelled out hysterically. "Calm down! I'm sure you're just upset because of the lightning," Chickery said.

"No! It's not the lightning, I swear somebody's outside!" "It's raining outside, and besides it may had been the shadows of a tree that you saw!" Chickery explained rationally. "Where are mom and dad?" Tommy asked unexpectedly. "I...I...I don't know," Chickery stuttered, "they were gone for ages. They probably went somewhere...they'll be back Tom, so relax!"

"No, no! Something's very wrong here!" Tommy screamed. "I think we have to go check up on Jake!" "ok, ok. We'll go check up on Jake," Chickery responded, rising up to his feet.

Following Tommy up the stairs, Chickery cuddled Wilbert and tried to cam down. They stood outside of Jake's bedroom and peered inside but oddly enough, Jake wasn't there except for the Tv screen which was still turned on.

"What on earth is going on?" Tommy screamed, "where is Jake?"

"Tommy, please calm down!" Chickery ordered, trying his best to remain calm but he was just as upset as his brother over the weird disappearance of his mown family.

"I can't calm down!" Tommy snapped. "How can we calm down when Jake is missing? Something strange is going on here, I know it is! Our family had disappeared and to make it worse, we have no clue as to where they'd went!"

"Will you please control yourself for just a moment...please?" Chikery yelled out, his mind spinning like crazy. "I'm upset over this, too. Just like you. But we need to calm down. Maybe mom and dad went for a walk. They'll be back!" "But that's crazy!" Tommy argued, "they wouldn't leave with out telling us! Besides, it's raining outside! Where would they go? And Jake's missing, too!" "I know, I know!" Chickery yelled back, "I am worried too. And yes I agree that something is going on here!" Tommy smirked. "At last we've actually agree on something!"

Chickery gave Tommy a stern glare. "Don't get cheeky with me, ok? Listen, there's no point in staying around and scaring ourselves this way. I say we go out and have a look around the neighborhood to find mom and dad." "Out there...when it's raining? Are you crazy?" Tommy exclaimed. "Great, then you can stay at home and take care of Wilbert while I go out and look for Mom and Dad!" Chickery snapped in annoyance as he turned and stormed out the door and downstairs.

There was the sound of thunder outside and he jumped in fright. The lights flickered several times then dimmed.

Suddenly, the lights went out and Chickery screamed, followed by Tommy. "That's it! I'm not staying inside this house another second!" Tommy cried out. "I'm going out with you!" Chickery blindly searched for the umbrella in the broom closet and as he and Tom neared the front door they heard a loud moan. "What on earth is that?" Tom asked breathlessly. Chickery swallowed hard. "I...I...I don't know...but come on. Let's go outside." Opening the front door, the two brothers tip toed out and there was another bolt of lightning.

They saw a dark figure in their driveway, lying on the ground and it was moaning loudly in pain.

"Oh my goodness!" Tommy cried. "I don't think we should go anywhere near it!"

"That may sound like a safe, sensible idea but we still can't ignore what's obviously lying in our driveway!" Chickery cried, walking timidly onto the front porch. "Why not ignore it?" Tommy cried hysterically. "It's raining and I don't think we should go outside like this. What if something happens to us?"

Chickery faced his brother, his eyes wide and angry. "Listen, Tommy. You can go ahead and stay here while I go out and look for mom and dad. That is, if it's what you want. But don't try to stop me from doing anything!"

Falling silent, Tommy stood helplessly on the front porch and watched as Chickery wondered down the driveway towards the dark figure.

"I still think you're crazy for doing this!" Chickery snapped.

As he stood before the dark heap in the driveway he could hear loud moaning coming from it, and he immediately staggered backwards.

He watched in terror as the figure squirmed and growled, only to go back to moaning once more.

Chickery shuddered in fear and turned around to go back inside when he recognized the face and his eyes widened. "Larry? Is that you?"

The lion slowly looked up from the ground and met Chickery's eyes steadily.

Chickery gasped when he saw blood oozing out of Larry's mouth.

There were bruises and scratches all over Larry and just seeing him in this state was enough to make Chickery feel immensely guilty for sending him out into the streets. "Oh my goodness! Come and help me please!" Chickery cried out to his brother. "Who is it?" Tommy yelled back. "Does it matter on who it is at this point?" Chickery cried in anguish. "Come on over and help me take him back into our house!"

As he waited for his brother to com over, Chickery shifted his focus to Larry who stared back at him in a dazed manner.

"Are you alright? What happened? Who did this to you?"

Larry's mouth twitched, and for several seconds he wasn't able to respond.

"I...I...I w-w-was...at...attacked while I was wondering around out here in the streets," he croaked out breathlessly.

"Oh, no! Not him again!" Tommy muttered when he realized on who it was.

"Tom! Be quiet, ok? Just help me get him inside our home! He's badly hurt!"

"What? Take him back inside our home...again?" Tom asked in disbelief.

"But surely, not after all that he'd done!"

"Tommy! Just be quiet and come on over and give me a hand would you?" Chikery hollered. Tommy rolled his eyes. "Fine. We'll help this idiot, again. And we'll take him back into our home...again, for the third time!"

Chickery flashed Tommy a dirty look. "Just focus on getting him inside for now would be great, Tom."

Tommy grunted and wobbled as he and Chickery tried in vain to lift Larry and carry him back to the patio but realized that the lion was simply too heavy.

"Phew! I don't think we can drag him back! I think he's eaten all of our food and so now he's damn fat!"

"Just keep trying!" Chickery snapped, "we can't just leave him out here to die! He's badly hurt!"

The two continued on dragging the heavy lion back to their front porch and what appeared to take for ever they finally managed to get the lion there in one piece. Tom, on the other hand, was breathless and pale. "I tell you what, this guy better be worth it," Tommy declared, "because he's caused enough problems as it is. Why on earth would you wanna help him?" "You sure ask a lot of questions," Chikery snapped. "Look, he's hurt. I think he should stay with us for awhile. And besides, I think he's changed." Tommy rolled his eyes. "Fine. What ever. But I still think you're making a mistake."

Moments later, Larry sat poised on the sofa, his deep wounds were bandaged and Chickery came downstairs with a blanket and pillows.

"You really are too kind to me," Larry gushed, "thanks so much for having me again. I really do appreciate it."

"Well, after I nearly fainted bringing you here, you should appreciate it," Tommy muttered bitterly.

Chickery gave Tommy a warning look. "Don't worry about thanking us. Just try and get better," he said to Larry.

"I would like to do something nice for you guys, I was thinking about cooking, how does that sound? Just to say thanks?"

"I wouldn't dare touch the food you dish up, heaven forbid, who knows what may exist in the food," Tommy declared sarcastically, "you could be putting poison into the food for all we both know!"

"I insist! Really, I do!" Larry pleaded relentlessly.

He tried to get up but cried out in pain and fell back down onto the sofa.

"That's it! You're not going anywhere, let alone cook anything!" Chickery confirmed, "concentrate on getting some rest, nothing else."

CHEE
CHE

"Honestly, have you gone nuts tonight?" Tommy demanded as he stomped upstairs. "I can't believe that creep is back in our home again, not after all that he's done!" "He's only staying for a little while," Chikery said, "and quit complaining already, ok? I'm tired. It's raining outside and we cannot go look for mom and dad in this weather. "So what? we just give up…like that?" Tommy asked incredulously. "Listen, if you want to go search outside then be my guest!" Chickery snapped, "but I'm going off to bed!" He went inside his bedroom and slammed the door. Tommy scowled angrily and went inside his own room and slammed the door shut. Meanwhile, Larry lay on the sofa, enjoying every second of the amusing commotion between the two brothers and he couldn't resist but to giggle at their petty quarrels. Suddenly, his stomach gurgled loudly and he cringed when he felt his insides squishing around. Patting his stomach, Larry's grin vanished and he grew very green in the face. He felt something push and kick violently in his stomach and he fell onto the floor in pain. He could feel something lurching up in his stomach. "Stop it! Stop this at once!" He ordered fiercely for the pain to stop but it didn't. It only grew worse. out of nowhere and quite unexpectedly, there was an echo of voices screaming and it sounded like it came from inside his stomach! "Let us out! Let us out…now!" The kicking and pushing continued and this time Larry felt very sick. He ran to the door and pulled it opened and from there he puked. But unfortunately the gross contents kept on gushing out–saliva, digested food particles and out came a large sized, disgusting looking ball that was his own digested food from two days ago–a ball coated in ice cream, saliva, pancakes and pizza. The ball came falling to the ground with a sickening, wet squishy sound. And then the ball itself went bouncing into the air, then stopped and bounced again. "Help us! Somebody help us get out of here!" The voices from inside the ball of puke cried out desperately. Larry knew exactly on who was inside the ball, and he swung back his feet and kicked the ball of puke out onto the wet streets, watching it with glee as it got washed down further down the streets in a flood of rain. "what are you doing?" A voice rung out from behind Larry. "why aren't you resting? who's at the door?" Larry spun around, appearing stunned but quickly composed when he realized it was only Tommy. Grinning his signature smirk, Larry shrugged and waved off Tommy's question dismissively. "oh, it's nobody."

Tommy raised his eyebrows questioningly. "Nobody at the door? Then why are you opening it?" Larry's grin became more forced and it stretched out wider, his eyes flashing red. "You really do ask a lot of questions, you know that? As I've said, there is no one out there. I was just simply… checking…that's all." Tommy snorted. "I don't believe you, but right now I don't really care. I reckon you're very weird." "I don't care what you think," Larry declared arrogantly, his eyes flashing dangerously, "You might want to go back to bed before something bad happens. And we don't want that, or do we?" "I wouldn't go around talking to people like that," Tommy shot back hotly, "You are staying inside my home and so if you dare do anything to me, Chikery would kick you out right away." Larry tossed back his head and laughed. "Your brother is under my spell, there is nothing you can do to stop me! Nothing at all, and he even took me back into his home! Isn't that great! We're always going to be friends for-ever!" Lifting up his bandaged arm, Larry's grin grew sinister. "You see this? I did this to myself, you know? All these wounds you see on me? I was the one who did them and your brother believed me!" Tommy gasped. "You little sneak! You creep! So this whole time, all this act in being in pain…it was all a lie?" Larry nodded. "Yes, of course. And you both fell for it. Now, you better go back to bed or else you may disappear too, like the rest of your family. I love small kids like you. You're so yummy and tasty, just like your brother Jake. oh, and then there's your parents…they're yummy too, but a bit too chewy. You how ever, will taste just perfect!" Tommy's face grew white in fear and his legs shook. "w-w…what did you do to my family? What did you do?" "oh, that's for you to find out yourself," Larry said mysteriously, "but I can tell you they're no longer in my stomach. oh, no! They're out there in the rain…probably being washed away to an island somewhere by now!" Tommy broke out in tears and he stomped his feet in anguish. "Tell me where my parents are right this instant!" Larry's face darkened. "You can yell all you want, but no one can know about this. It's our little secret! But then, who will believe you? Chickery won't believe you, he'll think you're crazy!" Suddenly, Chikery opened his bedroom door and went out. "what on earth is going on here?" Tommy gave Larry one last evil look before stomping back into his room, slamming the door shut. "what did you do to him?" Chickery demanded to Larry. Larry appeared very hurt. "I did nothing, I think he's just upset that your parents disappeared, that's all." "oh, no you don't," Chickery warned, "You're up to something, I can feel it." Larry cried out in pain and he staggered back into the living room. "I'm in pain right now, I will talk to you in the morning!" Chickery smacked his forehead in anger and stormed back to his room. Larry sunk deep into the couch and dragged the blankets up to his shoulders, a wicked grin on his face. "oh my poor dears, all alone and scared. But no fear, because by tomorrow I shall have you both for dessert. Hmmmm, yummy!" He licked his lips, and then an image of the kitten came to his mind. "oh, yes! And that goes for you too, Wilbert!"

Chickery groaned out loud to himself as he walked out the following morning since he was so sleepy and dazed. He wasn't able to drift off to sleep for the whole night due to the constant worries he had over his parent's disappearance.

Tommy got out of his room only seconds after his brother and he followed him downstairs in cold, stony silence. Chickery turned and forced a smile onto his face. "Good morning!" He cried out cheerfully. Tommy glared at Chickery and frowned. He muttered something to himself but then stared down at the floor. Sighing in irritation at Tommy's behavior, chcikery decided to avoid any possible arguments in the morning by ignoring Tommy and going down the rest of the staircase when he suddenly caught the wonderful aroma of something cooking coming from the kitchen. Curious, he and Tommy wondered over to the kitchen and they stood speechlessly at the doorway, watching in silence as Larry prepared breakfast at the stove. "I see somebody made a speedy recovery," Tommy remarked dryly. Larry spun around and he broke out into a slow, weak grin. "Good morning, there. Come on in and sit at the table. Breakfast's almost ready." chikery frowned and crossed his arms as he stared at Larry, his eyes twinkled in suspicion. "I thought you were in pain? But I have to agree with Tommy that you may have recovered a lot faster than we've thought." Tommy rolled his eyes. "That depends if he was ever in any such pain from the start." Larry remained silent for awhile before he responded. "Yes, I am in serious pain...but I'm so grateful for what you've done for me last night and so this is the best I could do to thank you...," Larry fell silent once more but this time not for long. He flashed Tommy an odd look. "Why not come in and have some breakfast? You look like you could use something to eat." "oh, how very kind," Tommy muttered sarcastically, "but no thanks. I am having some cereal." chikery walked over to Larry and helped prepare the finishing touches of their breakfast. "You know, this really isn't necessary," he started, "but... thanks anyways. It's lovely." Larry smiled. "No problem. we are still friends, right?" chikery didn't reply and instead grabbed the bowels and brought them over to the table.

"I'm nearly finished with the soup," Larry informed, stirring the pot with a wooden spoon. "It should be ready soon." Larry gazed in hunger at the two brothers seated at the table and he licked his lips. He was distracted when wilbert entered the room. Smiling wickedly, Larry abandoned the pot, dumping the spoon into it as it boiled away at the stove. Larry's stomach grumbled. This is it! He thought excitedly to himself.

Larry wondered over to the table with slow, deliberate steps.

The pot was boiling away at the stove and the soup was gushing over the pot, creating hissing noises as it dripped onto the hotplate.

Wilbert stood inches away from Larry, watching his every move with large fearful eyes. Larry gave it a wicked smile.

"Oh, great. Looks like today is another wet day," Chickery commented, looking out at the window at his table.

Tommy shrugged his shoulders and went on eating his cereal in silence.

None of them paid Larry any attention. They both were too busy munching down their breakfast.

Larry licked his lips and got closer to Chickery, his sharp claws extended and moving closer towards his neck. Wilbert meowed loudly at the scenario and this caused Tommy to look up. His eyes widened and he stood up quickly, causing his bowel to topple over and shattered to the floor. "Chickery! Look out! Be careful!" Chickery looked confused. "W-what are you talking about?" "Meeeeeooooow!" Suddenly Wilbert leaped into the air and clawed at Larry, causing the lion to stumble backwards and collapsed to the floor.

Chickery turned to stare and watched in horror as Larry clawed at the kitten, wrestling it off him!

"Larry! Stop it! Stop at once!" Chickery cried, "he's only a kitten! You're hurting him!" But Larry went on fighting Wilbert off him, and when he failed to do so, he got hold of Wilbert's tail and bit into it hard. Wilbert screeched in pain and Larry got hold of its tail and flung the poor creature out of the kitchen.

Chickery screamed in fright. He ran after the kitten but Wilbert had already scurried off elsewhere in the house.

"How can you do that to him?" Chickery snapped, "he's only a kitten! That's it! I want you out! Get out!" Tommy smirked. "I told you this guy was bad news. Maybe now you'll believe me!" "Oh, just be quiet, ok Tom?" Chickery snapped, "come and help me look for Wilbert." He gave Larry a final, cold stare. "I never want to see you ever again! Now leave!"

The brothers left the kitchen but Tommy turned to smirk at Larry before disappearing into the hallway.

Larry's face darkened and he balled up his fists.

He'd forgotten all about the stove, which was now alight with fire.

The soup was bubbling away feverishly and the soup was spouting down onto the hotplate heavily and dark smoke clouded the kitchen.

"Wilbert? Wilbert, where are you?" Chickery asked frantically in the hallway. "It's ok, boy. I'm here. Please come out." Tommy couldn't resist smirking to himself as he watched his brother get down onto his knees and searched every corner, nook and cranny of their home in the search for Wilbert. "You know, none of this would happen if only you had listened to me in the first place," he declared arrogantly. "I told you Larry was bad news. But, of course you didn't listen to me. You never do!" Chickery's topped his search and spun around angrily, his eyes flashing. "Listen, I'm tired to death of you constantly reminding me about Larry. Ok, fine. So you are right, there...is that what you you're dying to hear?" "Hey! Don't get mad at me, ok?" Tommy shot back, "this isn't my fault. I'm just saying that I've tried to help you but you wouldn't listen. And besides, he was very close to eating you and I saved you...," "Oh, right. As usual, you want to be the hero, don't you?" Chickery yelled back, his face red. "Well, guess what? You're not anything. Not a famous boxer, nor a hero. Just a pain in my neck at the moment! And for your information, Larry would never eat me. He just wouldn't." "Oh, really? If it wasn't for me, he'd have you chewed up by now," Tommy raved on, "you don't know who you're dealing with. This guy's is not a true friend. He's lied to you and he faked his own injuries." "I know Larry perfectly well, so thanks for reminding me!" Chickery retorted, "so why don't you be quiet and come help me look for...," he trailed off mid sentence and sniffed the air deeply and he grew pale. "What is that burning smell? Isn't that the smell of something burning? What is that smell!" Larry appeared in the hallway. Chickery saw him and felt annoyed. "What are you still doing here? I told you to leave. So go on...get out." Larry's eyes twinkled mischievously and his eyes mouth curled up in a cruel smile. "I'm not going anywhere. I'm staying right here!" "Excuse me?" Chikery asked, raising his eyebrows. "I remember telling you to leave." Suddenly that strong odor of dark smoke flooded into the hallway and the brothers coughed. "Oh, my goodness! What have you done?" Tommy cried, coughing loudly. "What's burning?"

Larry didn't move but that smile grew more sinister with each passing minute. "It's over now, kids. I've won this battle. Smart, aren't I? Game over. You're all mine and I'm going to eat you...right now!" Larry ran to them and he opened his mouth wide and roared. Chikery and Tommy screamed and staggered away and he accidentally knocked Tommy to the floor. Tommy collapsed to the floor with a loud thud and there he would lie extremely still. "Tommy! Get up! We have to leave!" But Tommy lay motionless on the floor and said nothing. Chickery grew very shaky. The dark heavy smoke flooded into the hallway and Chikery coughed. Somewhere from inside the house he could make out meowing noises but before he could break out in joy, Larry's cruel, cold laughter burst into the air. "You're all mine now!" He declared, licking his lips hungrily.

Larry wondered over to Chickery and those red eyes fixed directly at him. "You made a mistake, you know that?" Larry asked, his voice soft and sarcastic. "You made me very angry. Should have left me alone. But, noooo…you had to trick me into being your friend. well, nobody tricks me! Nobody! Do you hear me? You're going to pay with your life!" "I didn't do anything!" Chickery snapped, backing off to the nearby broom closet. "All I wanted was to be your friend. That is all I wanted, was for us to be friends!" "well, I didn't want to be friends!" Larry yelled, roaring at the top of his lungs. "You should've left me alone. But you didn't. You fooled me into thinking that I'm your friend, and that you cared about me. very bad mistake, you know that?" "You're such a loser, you know that?" Chickery spat out venomously, "so, you want to be alone? That is fine. Just fine with me. Go ahead and be alone for the rest of your life. I did you a favor by being friends with you! You big fat loser!" Larry's eyes flashed dangerously. "How dare you call me a loser? I'm going to destroy you right now! I ate your parents, along with your brother Jake. So, now there are only three of you!" Chickery gasped. "You ate my family? How could you!" "what can I say? They make a very tasty meal indeed!" Larry cackled. By now the hallway felt very hot and they could barely see each other over the thick dark smoke that was swooping around them. But Chickery could feel the lion's presence staring before him, he felt that presence coming closer and he gripped the closet door opened and grasped onto a mop handle. The thick smoke stung his eyes and he coughed heavily. "say good-bye, good old Chickery!" Larry snarled, "you'll die right now!" Chcikery swung the mop handle into the air and it narrowly missed Larry's head. Larry roared in surprise and swiftly got hold of the mop and broke it into pieces before leaping into the air. Laughing hysterically, Larry swiped his claws at Chickery, ripping into his flesh. Chickery hollered in pain. He knew that this was it. He was going to die! Tears dripping down his face, Chickery closed his eyes and prepared to be eaten. As Larry dug another set of claws into Chikery, a sudden crash occurred and Larry roared in pain. Chickery opened his eyes and saw Larry fall to the floor, collapsing in a heap, surrounded by shards of broken glass fragments from a vase of broken glass fragments from a vase. Tommy got hold of his brother's arms and dragged him through the thick smoke. "come on! we need to get out of here!" Tommy cried, coughing and wheezing. "No! No! No!" Chikery yelled back stubbornly, "we need to go find Wilbert! I'm not leaving with-out him!"

"Don't be so crazy for once in your life!" Tommy snapped, waving smoke away from his face. "We need to save ourselves first! Just forget about Wilbert! We need to get out...now!" "I said no!" Chikery yelled back, coughing. "We need to go find Wilbert! I am not leaving until we find him!" Making his way through the thick smoke, Chickery coughed and squinted as his eyes began to water. "Meeoooow! Meooooow!" "Wilbert!" Chickery cried out in happiness. "Where are you? Answer me!" The meowing continues once more and he realized that it was coming from upstairs. "Come on, let's get out of here!" Tommy pleaded in frustration and annoyance. "Please, hurry up! We need to get out right now!" Ignoring his brother, Chickery ran up the staircase and found himself tripping several times due to the smoke preventing him from seeing where he was going but he forced himself to make it all the way to the top landing despite his aching pains. Chickery spotted a shadow among the dark clouds of smoke and he kneeled down to touch on what could possibly be Wilbert. The shadow meowed frantically and he burst out laughing in relief. Scooping the terrified kitten into his arms, he turned to head downstairs but the entire hallway and staircase was now alight in fire! Lost and terrified out of his mind, Chickery's mind couldn't function any longer and he felt the room spinning like crazy. The smoke was hurting his eyes and his vision as he felt the ferocious heat blowing into his face and he could no longer breathe. But weak as he may felt, he quickly dashed into his bedroom and slammed the door. He could hear somebody crying out his name but his mind was so foggy now and he had to leave this house by jumping out of his bedroom window! Crazy as it may sound, at the moment, he had no choice. He cuddled Wilbert and scurried over to his window and yanked it open and then hastily threw out a couple of pillows to the ground. "I'm so sorry boy. But you need to go out first!" Taking a deep breath, he lifted Wilbert into the air and threw him out of the window, feeling terrible as he heard the kitten's hoarse screeching. By now the smoke and fire was catching up at the top of the staircase and billows of smoke seeped beneath the door. Paralyzed with fear, Chickery couldn't move except to look out the window and to his relief he spotted Wilbert had safely landed on the ground and had ran off. He heard loud crackling and his back felt like it was on fire! Turning around, he screamed as the wooden door melted like burnt paper and it collapsed to the floor, just as a bolt of fire poured into the room!

"oh goodness! somebody helllllp!" chickery hollered hoarsely, coughing and closing his eyes as the tremendous blazing heat washed over him. He felt his whole body burning and his eyes were hurting like crazy.Everything suddenly became dark black and he couldn't see anything anymore. Confused and with his mind spinning like crazy, he turned to the window and started to climb over the ledge but as he looked down from the great height he froze. The raging fire was by now sweeping into the room and he felt his whole body burning ands his eyes were stinging like crazy! Everything suddenly became a dark black and he wasn't able to see but he turned towards the window, forcing himself to feel brave, to have the courage to jump out of the window. He felt the fire spreading all over his room and the smoke was making it very hard to breathe. But among the fires and burns he felt somebody's presence. Somebody was in this room with him! But...who could it be? He felt this person wondering slowly over to him. He could recognize the familiar raspy, heavy breathing and he heard the menacing growl. He cried out in pain as he felt sharp claws digging into his wounds. Realizing that he had no choice, chikery scrambled onto the window ledge but felt sharp teeth sinking into him and he hollered in sheer pain and the next thing he knew he was tumbling out of the window.He didn't know when he landed onto the pillows on the ground, the fall had been fast and now he felt so much pain. "Help meeeeee! somebody help, please!" He wailed frantically as he looked around but all he saw was pitch blackness. "Chickery! oh, goodness! There you are!" Tommy's voice rung out in joy and relief. Tommy got hold of his brother and tried to lift him to his feet but chickery cried out in pain. "Stop! I'm in pain!" He declared feveri   shly. "well, you're going to have to try!" Tommy yelled back, "come on! The house is on fire! I need you to get up!" "I can't! I'm in so much pain!" chickery declared. "Save yourself!" There was silence for a moment. "Just wait here," Tommy instructed, "I'll be back!" "where are you going?" chickery asked frantically but there was no answer Moments later Tommy pushed the wheelbarrow out onto the lawn. "ok, I got the wheelbarrow from the shed," Tommy confirmed, "I'll get you into it!" Grunting, he assisted his brother into the wheelbarrow the best he could but Tommy lost his balance and chickery collapsed into the wheelbarrow and he gasped in shock. His head made into contact with the edge of the wheelbarrow and he became unconscious! "oh my goodness! chickery! wake up! can you hear me?" Tommy demanded. He looked at his brother lying in the wheelbarrow and felt very hopeless. He glared up at the house and gasped when he saw that the house was now on fire! Dark smoke was blowing out of the windows and Tommy shrieked when the glass windows shattered and parts of the house were falling down!

Tommy jumped into action and quickly pushed the wheelbarrow straight ahead, narrowly missing the debris that was falling down.

Coughing heavily, Tommy used all his strength and pushed the wheelbarrow down the driveway and onto the road. Feeling dazed and tired, Tommy gasped for breath and forged down the street but he was hardly halfway there when he had to stop and catch his breath. Suddenly, there was a monstrous explosion occurring from behind him and the sound was so deafening and powerful that he felt a forceful push from behind. He collapsed into the wheelbarrow and shielded his head with his arms for protection. He could feel debris and pebbles landing onto his body, head and arms. The sound of the explosion whistled through the air and Tommy lay still, paralyzed in fear. He cried out in pain as more debris landed into him. Looking up shakily, he turned to stare over his shoulder and was shocked to see that his beautiful home was now gone. Completely burned to the ground. Crying miserably, Tommy turned to Chickery and shook him fiercely. "Wake up! Wake up! Please! We've lost our home! I need you to wake up...Now!" Tommy realized in dismay that Chickery wasn't going to wake up anytime soon and so he helped his unconscious brother with both arms and carried him down the street. "Are we going somewhere?" A voice rung out from behind. Looking over his shoulder, Tommy's eyes widened when he spotted a hideous creature meters away from him. The animal was badly burned, with serious cuts and open wounds all over its body. Tommy immediately recognized that it was Larry and he screamed. "Stay away from me! Tommy ran ahead, clutching Chikery the best he could but the heavy weight was getting to him. Looking back, he saw Larry stumbling through the mountains of debris, his eyes well focused on Tommy. Larry continued on wondering ahead but he didn't see the wheelbarrow that obstructerd his path until it was too late and he fell on top of it before breaking out in a furious roar. "Help! Somebody help me!" Tommy cried, running around the neighborhood but nobody cared enough to come out and help. Tommy ran to the near-by park that was about a block away from his neighborhood, losing his breath and energy fast but he still pushed himself in forging ahead. He made the grave mistake of looking back over his shoulder, obviously fearful and paranoid over Larry might possibly catching up with him that he didn't see the large stacks of tree branches and logs littering the ground ahead of him until he felt his feet flipping into the air and he lost grip of his brother and watched in horror as Chickery sailed into the air and his lifeless body rolled down the steep hill. At the bottom of that steep hill was a lake and Tommy's eyes widened as Chickery's body rolled right into the lake and got washed away down the small stream!

Tommy was breathing heavily as he watched Larry collapsed onto the ground, still clutching onto the heavy tree branch but this time he felt the situation was very different—this time, he had something to protect himself with, he'd got protection in using this tree branch and he didn't feel scared in the least. This time, Tommy understood that he was the one in charge and was the powerful one and it sure felt good! Panting excitedly, Tommy glared down at Larry's crumpled body writhing on the ground and he realized that while the lion was hurt, he was still alive!

"See what I mean? I told you I wasn't scared of you anymore," Tommy muttered out softly, "and I did promise that I could've hurt you but as usual you didn't believe in a damn thing I've said. So how dies it feel now? Not being the tough one anymore?" Larry moaned and growled in anger, clutching his face and tossed and turned in agony. "You one dumb fool! You shouldn't have done that! I'm going to get you for this!"

"Oh, I don't think you're in any position to be threatening anybody at the moment," Tommy shot back, smirking and swinging the branch back and forth. "Now, I need to go find my brother and so you better back off or else I'll hurt you again, I will hurt you. Trust me on that. You don't scare me anymore." "Fine, ok! ok! You win!" Larry declared coldly, "and so just relax and chill out. Trust me on this. I've given up. I will leave you alone I promise!" Tommy sighed slowly and gave ount a hand to help Larry to his feet. "Maybe you should talk like that more often and not be so aggressive all the time" "You're so damn stupid, just like your brother!" Larry snarled arrogantly, "seriously, can't believe you fell for that! You're far more silly than I'd thought!" Tommy's hopes sank deeply and his eyes widened. "Oh, no. Not again! You tricked me!" "Yes and your brother tricked me!" Larry exclaimed, "now it's your turn to pay up!"

Larry roared and leaped into the air whilst Tommy staggered backwards, clutching the tree branch for dear life.

Larry got hold of Tommy's neck and started digging his claws into his flesh. "Prepare to be eaten to pieces now, my sweet one," Larry whispered in a sinister tone.

Tommy thrashed his arms wildly, hoping to take another swipe at Larry by using the branch but this time he was the loser–Larry once again was the stronger one and he had to save himself fast before he had his breath knocked out of him!

Tommy tried to thump Larry with the branch but the lion was too quick for him and got hold of Tommy's fist and knocked the branch out of his grip.

"Not so fast little one!" Larry cooed sweetly, tightening his claws around Tommy's neck.

Tommy's face grew pale and he fought the best he could but he realized he was no match for Larry's strength!

As Tommy struggled to breathe, the world began to spin wildly and he began to see stars dancing in front of him.

He felt his body growing weaker as he struggled to breathe and his head hung to the ground, that was when he noticed Larry's serious open wounds on both feet.

Feeling a surge of hope flash before him, Tommy lifted his feet and began to stomp down onto Larry's bleeding wounds, watching in satisfaction as Larry let go and roared in pain.

Larry started to reach out for his feet and comfort his own wounds but Tommy gave another strong thump on the foot and Larry roared in agony.

The lion fell to the ground and went on roaring while Tommy took this chance to run for his life!

He ran down towards the stream in the lake, hoping to find Chickery but his brother was nowhere in sight, and he realized a search hunt was in order.

He ran down the long dirt path, following the lake's trail and he finally saw a body afloat in the water at the end of the lake.

Crying out in happiness, Tommy ran towards the end of the lake and tried to pull his brother out of the water, looking over his shoulder to make sure Larry wasn't behind him. Larry was nowhere in sight.

Grunting, Tommy dragged his brother away from the lake and then lifted him over his shoulder before he took off into the other directions into the dark woods. For what appeared to take for ever, he scurried through the woods and Tommy finally stumbled across a clear path that leads to the cab ranks!

Excited, he scrambled towards the line of cabs parked in a long queue hoping to catch a ride but he saw a beefy driver seated inside the first cab, glaring coldly at him. "Listen, I need a ride to the hospital fast, my brother's badly hurt!" Tommy explained. "If you have the money then hop in," the cold driver informed, "or else get lost!" "There's a dangerous lion somewhere out there and he tried to hurt us, please help us!"

Tommy begged desperately.(

"I'm sorry to hear that, I really do but there's no such thing as a free ride my boy," the driver snapped, "either you pay up or get out of here!" "Fine, then just call for an ambulance please!" Tommy demanded. "Just call for help!" "Don't take orders from a kid, but considering this is a serious emergency...", the driver grumbled in annoyance as he started to call 911 on his cell phone. Tommy got over to the side of the door and opened it and placed Chickery seated upwards. "Hey! Hey! The ambulance is coming, get him out! This is a cab, not a hospital!" The beefy driver cried out angrily, getting out of the driver seat and tried to grab Tommy out of the back passenger seat but Tommy scurried onto the driver's seat and started the engine. The cab driver backed off, shocked by Tommy's actions. "Don't you dare do that! Get out now!" But Tommy ignored the driver and stamped onto the gas pedal and lurched backwards, crashing into the cabs behind him. Various other cabs from behind honked their horns in protest and cried out. Tommy changed the gears and sped away from the ranks while the driver ran after him, yelling out threats. When Tommy got to the intersection, he stopped and took a deep breath and then laughed out loud. He was actually the one driving the cab, he couldn't believe it! He realized in shock that he hadn't closed his door nor the passenger door either and as he was about to get out and shut both doors, he saw the driver running breathlessly towards the cab and out of panic Tommy drove forward a few inches when a scared kitten ran out onto the road and stopped in front of his cab! Braking unexpectedly and with tires screeching, Tommy tried to get a hold of himself as he glared at the kitten and he realized it was Wilbert! Gesturing towards the kitten, Tommy quickly scooped it up into his arms and he laid the cat into the side seat before closing the door. "Oh, I miss you boy, so very much!" Tommy declared, "hold on tight ok? We need to get out of here!"

Tommy started to drive off down the road and before long he was out into the busy open road with other agitated drivers but this time Tommy felt safe. Larry was gone and all Tommy had to focus on was getting his brother to hospital. Turning to a frightened and dazed Wilbert, Tommy broke out in a smile. "We're safe now, boy. It's all good now." But Wilbert's eyes bulged and it yelped out. "What's wrong, boy? Are you hurt?" Tommy declared, feeling very alarmed. He noticed that Wilbert was glaring out of Tommy's window, staring at somebody...or something. Tommy turned to stare and he gasped when he saw Larry driving a cab directly in the second lane. "Oh, no! No! No! Not you again!"

Tommy sunk deeper into his seat, but he was unable to look away at the horrifying sight that greeted his very eyes!

Larry's eyes were cold and distant, but his snarl curled up into a sinister smirk. "It looks like we've meet again...my dear pal."

Tommy shook his head in disbelief. "B-b-but...t...t...this is impossible! what are you doing still alive?" "what can I say?" Larry shrugged, "I have nine lives. Did you think that a stupid tree branch was supposed to destroy me? You're more stupid and more of idiot than I'd thought you were!"

"I'm warning you, back off!" Tommy hollered, "or else you're going to be sorry! stay away!" "what are you going to do to me this time?" Larry taunted eagerly, "run me over with your car? Lets not forget, I have one too."

Tommy braced himself and focused on the road ahead of him.

It was time to keep a move on, that much was for sure, especially if he wanted to make it alive! Tommy stomped onto the gas pedal and drove off straight ahead but the open road was now beginning to become crowded and busy and he had no choice but to serve past the long queues of cars just to keep driving ahead but before he could breathe in relief he saw an oncoming bus turning into his lane and he almost froze over in shock. Hundreds of cars beeped their horns and the bus driver frantically waved at him to brake. The bus driver came to a sudden stop, while tires screeched but Tommy swerved back into the available lane on the left, nearly colliding into that lane's oncoming traffic. The bus driver stuck his head out and pounded his fist into the air. "You flaming lunatic!"

Tommy continued on driving, not knowing on where he was to go.

As he came to a stop at a red light, he glared over to the side and spotted a large bulletin sign that indicated there was a circus in town about half a mile away.

Feeling excited, Tommy knew that this was the best way to avoid Larry by driving to a place that is loaded with crowds! They wouldn't be able to get caught in a large crowd like that... Tommy drove another couple of blocks on the road until he spotted a noisy commotion occurring from the streets ahead and saw that he'd reached the circus.

Braking suddenly at the side of the road only meters away from the entrance gates of the circus, Tommy killed off the engine and got over to the backseat.

"chikcery! wake up, now! we've got to go...right this instant!"

Tommy shifted his weight and with one available hand he grasped onto the doorknob and pulled but unfortunately the door wouldn't budge! "What on earth is going on here?" Tommy hollered out in disbelief and frustration, pulling the doorknob fiercely but to his shock the damn door knob collapsed into his hand and he almost lost grip of Chikery and collide down the staircase! "What's going on here?" Chickery asked in a dazed manner, his face tilting from side to side but he had no idea what he was seeing since he could no longer see. Tommy held the door knob in his hand and shook his head in disbelief. "The door know fell off! What on earth are we supposed to do, now?" "Well, surely we can go back down and find someplace else to hide!" Chickery suggested weakly while Wilbert meowed hysterically, obviously even the kitten could feel the anxiety going on in the atmosphere and was clearly upset too. Tommy flashed his brother a cold look, despite the guy not being able to see. "Geez, now that's a great idea, isn't it? Now, why haven't I thought of that? Don't be ridiculous! Larry could be waiting downstairs right now as we speak!" Chickery crossed his arms and pouted. "No need to be so rude, ok? I was only trying to help!" "Well, you would help a lot more if you can come up with a better idea rather than throwing us into more trouble! I think we have no choice but to knock this door down!" "Well, now that's a great idea!" Chickery agreed sarcastically, "and what exactly is hiding on the other side of the damn door?" "Do I look like a magician?" Tommy snapped rudely, "seriously, I just hope there is another set of rooms on the others side because we cannot head back downstairs at this point!" Tommy let go of Chickery and started heaving his body weight against the door, startling both Chickery and Wilbert. "Easy! Easy! Come on, you'll break the damn thing!" Chickery scolded in disapproval. "Well, do you have any better ideas? Just top lecturing me and help me already!" Chikery sighed and started throwing his weight against the door frame, joining force with his brother as they went on heaving against the door various times before the door itself would abruptly open with a loud rusty squeaking sound. Standing side by side, the brothers stared out into the horrendous view before them, their eyes wide opened in horror. Instead of looking into a set of rooms as they had hoped for originally, they were staring out into a spacious balcony equipped with a long steel rail and from their distance they could see partial views of the bottom ground. Tommy felt like he was about to go hysterical with madness. "No, no, no! This cannot be what's in store for us! I won't accept this! I just won't!" Chickery and Wilbert watched Tommy jump up and down in agony and both couldn't find anything to do except to stare and feel helpless. To their horror, they could spot a dark figure sweeping from the bottom and within seconds they heard thundering footsteps pounding upstairs and they froze in absolute terror. Larry climbed the rest of the stairs and his eyes gleamed. "I see my precious little piglets have nowhere else to hide, that's great! We're all here! Now, get ready to die!" Tommy, Chickery and Wilbert huddled together and screamed our in terror, trembling like leaf caught in a blizzard.

Tommy and Chickery staggered backwards against the railing, feeling totally helpless. Wilbert followed suite and tried to hide behind Chickery but he had his back pressed against the railing and so there wasn't enough room for Wilbert to hide. Larry smirked in amusement as he witnessed their fear. "There's no need to be scared my precious dears," he said sweetly, all the while that sinister snarl never left his scarred face. "I promise I'll make this quick and simple. You guys won't feel a damn thing!" "Why are you doing this?" Chickery wailed hysterically. "We haven't done anything to you! If anything, we've been very good to you! We gave you a place to stay and we fed you too! Is this how you're planning on repaying us for our kindness and generosity?" "I never asked for anything, especially nothing from you!" Larry snapped coldly, his yes blazing in anger, "I've told you from the beginning that I wanted you to leave me alone! I didn't want to be friends with you, but you had to go and trick me into believing that you guys are my friends, my family! Well, I don't like being tricked! Do you hear me? You shouldn't have messed around with me, because I won't let you get away with it! I'm no fool, and so how dare you try to make me look foolish? Did you really think that I was that stupid?" "Well, from the looks of things, maybe you really are everything you've just said!" Tommy declared bravely, "My brother did something very nice for you. He gave you a great friendship, he cared about you! He tried to make your life a whole lot less lonely by being your friend, and this is how you show your gratitude? What a loser! Maybe he really should have ignored you, left you feeling lonely. Creeps like you don't deserve friends!" Larry's eyes flashed dangerously. "You can say all you want, because it isn't going to change anything. I'm still going to eat all three of you right now. I've been waiting for this, you know? Been dying to gobble all three of you and now it looks like I may get my wish!" Tommy turned and stared at Chikery and they both nodded silently, both understanding one another's plan. "You are going to have a hard time eating all of us," Tommy stated smugly, "because we won't be standing in one place...we'll be everywhere and you're going to have to chase us...if you can!" With out another minute wasted, Tommy darted to the left side of the balcony while Chickery ran off to the right side, clutching Wilbert. Larry cackled evilly. "Ohhh, you're making me so much hungrier! You wanna play games? Ok, let's begin!" Larry charged at Tommy as his first choice and Tommy ran off and Larry narrowly missed him and collided into the railing. The railing shook due to the heavy impact and Tommy took this chance to be charging directly into Larry with all the force he could manage. The lion roared in surprise as he was pushed back against the delicate railing, while the steel railing itself clattered noisily. The screws slowly fell right off its joints and the railing collapsed down the balcony and to Tommy's roared out in protest as his body sailed slowly into the air while Chikery still hung onto him, both were too stunned to realize what had happened. Tommy quickly ran up to his brother and snatched at Chikery's shirt, pulling him back slight while Larry's loud roar echoed through out the air as his body fell down onto the ground. The brothers heard a loud thud as Larry hit the ground and there were silence as Tommy tried to get his brother back onto the balcony but due to his haste Chickery's shirt started to rip and to his horror Chickery fell backwards and nearly toppled down into the ground. He luckily managed to grab hold of the ledge of the balcony. Wilbert meowed hysterically while Chickery's face grew a ghastly white, just like a ghost!

Chikery felt his mind spinning like crazy as he felt the weight of his body floating into the air and he almost choked himself as fear got the better of him and he felt himself growing dizzy in the process. Don't look down, please...what ever you do...just don't look down...ever! He silently ordered himself and he squeezed his eyes shut as fear took over and he hollered at the top of his lungs! "Helllllp! Oh my gosh, please! Somebody come and help me!" There were loud gasps coming from below, and before he knew it there were people screaming. Tommy dashed over hesitantly to the ledge and kneeled down. His hands shook violently as he extended his hand. "Quick! Grab hold of me! Come on, Chikery!"

Chikery opened his eyes and slowly grasped onto Tommy's hand but he slowly felt his fingers began to slip off the edge of the balcony and he screamed even harder. "Nooooo! I think I'm going to fall! Don't let me fall! Whatever you do...just don't let me go...please!" "I won't! I won't! I promise!" Tommy shrieked hysterically, his face breaking out in a cold sweat and turning blue as he felt his body slipping forward closer over the ledge and Chikery realized this and he grew even more frantic. "Don't let me fall!" "I don't think I can hold on for much longer...Chikery!" Tommy gasped out desperately, breathing breathlessly, pulling harder onto his brother's hand backwards as hard as he could but his body was being dragged forward. "Hold on up there!" A voice hollered from the bottom, "Hold onto each other and I'll come on up!" Tommy felt his whole body breaking out in immense relief. Finally, help was coming! Loud footsteps pounded up the staircase and Tommy's relief took over and he felt his grip began to loosen and Chikery screamed at the top of his lungs. "Don't let me go!" Wilbert meowed and began to climb onto Tommy's back, clawing him in fright. "Get off me, Wilbert! You aren't helping!" Tommy barked in annoyance.

Suddenly, a burly tall man got over to the two brothers and with a loud grunt, he dragged Chickery upwards and within seconds Chikery was pulled back onto the balcony, away from the edge. Breathing and coughing, the two brothers threw themselves into a hug and began to cry. "Thank God you're ok!" Tommy cried out loud, "I thought I almost lost you!" "I'm ok, I'm ok!" Chickery reassured excitedly, "shhhhhhhh, it's all going to be ok now...our nightmare is over!" "Are you two alright?" The stranger asked, his face frowning in concern, "do you need to go to hospital?" "No, that won't be necessary," Chickery confirmed, "we are fine. None of us are hurt...but there is just one thing..." "Oh, no...don't tell me Larry is back," Tommy groaned. "No, I don't think he is going to come back up, he's probably in serious pain. But we still have to find mom and dad...and Jake. This isn't over yet!"

"But that's impossible! We don't even know where they are yet!" Tommy pointed out, "They could be just about anywhere!" Chikery sighed. "Yeah, that's my point. I just don't know what to do anymore. But let's hurry up and leave this place. Since I almost died up here I want to get away from this place as soon as possible!"

"Yeah, I agree, let's get off this balcony!" Tommy agreed, beckoning Wilbert to follow as the two brothers guided each other out the door while the man scooped Wilbert into his arms and carried him downstairs. Moments later all four of them stood outside the large mirror house and in front of Larry's body, which was curled up in a heap. Tommy looked down at the creature uneasily. "Is he dead?" "No, he isn't dead yet," the man confirmed, pointing at the creature's body. "See? He's still breathing." "Well, that is not good news at all!" Tommy snapped, "What if he tries to get back at us again? We almost got killed!" "Tommy, calm down!" Chikery scolded, "Listen, the man's right. Larry isn't dead yet. But our worst nightmare is over now. Besides, look at him! He's badly hurt. He needs to go straight to hospital!" "I think we should leave him here!" Tommy argued, "After all, take a look at all that he's done to us! We were almost killed!" "But while he's still alive, we need to get him into hospital for treatment," the man explained patiently. "The crowd of people standing outside must have contacted the paramedics because it should be coming over soon." The crowd of people was still standing outside by the gates, some had even started to wonder back inside but they didn't dare come any closer. Chikery went over to Tommy and embraced his brother, followed by Wilbert. For a moment, none of them said a word, until Tommy spoke up. "We can't go back home because the house had burnt down…so where would we sleep?" Chikery closed his eyes as the painful memory of his house burning in the raging fired crept back into his mind. "I don't know, Tommy. I just don't know anymore." Minutes later the paramedics came and Larry was placed onto a stretcher and was boarded into the van. The crowd began to wonder off slowly and the four of them stood together glaring at the paramedics van as it drove off, its bright lights trailed in the night's sky. Suddenly, without warning, a middle aged woman came running into the carnival's ground, looking all flushed and breathless. "Hey, excuse me lady, but you really shouldn't be here," the man informed, starting to guide her away by the elbow, "the carnival's closed due to what's happened…I'm sure you must've seen what's happened." The lady pulled herself free from the man's grasp. "Yes, I did indeed see what happened. But I'm one of the workers here at the carnival," she touched her silky red blouse, "can't you see that I'm a gypsy? I can see your future right now if you want." Chickery and Tommy stared at each other warily and almost cracked up laughing. "Thanks, but no thanks…I think I would have a very nice future," the man said sarcastically. He turned to the brothers and waved. "You guys take care ok? All the best." With out another word, the man walked off into the night. The gypsy stuck out her tongue at the man's back. "Yes, I sure hope he'll have a nice life, indeed." She turned to the boys and rubbed her hands together, her eyes gleaming. "Now, what about you two? You want me to show you what's going to happen in the next few days?"

Tommy and Chickery glared at each other, looking very annoyed and bewildered. "Listen, we don't mean to be rude," Chikery started to say, "but considering we were nearly killed, I think we're both too tired to be looking into our future at the moment...but thanks anyways." Turning to his brother, Chikery hugged him and then onto Wilbert. "We better get going and find a place to stay for tonight." The lady bustled after them, dancing merrily. "Are you guys trying to find a place to sleep for tonight?" "Yes, we are," Tommy sighed impatiently, "if you don't mind it's been a very crazy day and so let's all go." "Well, I was about to offer you boys a place to stay at my place," the woman said slowly, "...but I guess you boys won't be interested...so I'll go..." Tommy immediately lit up. "Really? You are offering us a place to stay?" "But what do you expect in return from us?" Chickery asked, feeling very suspicious. "I mean...you don't even know us!" "Well, geez...all I want is to do something nice for the two of you after all that's happened, there's no need to think the worst of me!" "I'm sorry to do that, its just that we are all shaken up after all that's happened, " Chickery explained, "but if your offer still stands, we would love to take up on it." The woman burst out smiling. "Great, then follow me. The tent is this way down the street from here." Chickery raised his eyebrows questioningly. "Excuse me? A tent? But there are three of us!" "Oh, stop worrying and follow me! It's a very big tent! Besides, we have to look for your parents first." "You know where my parents are?" Chikery asked, astonished. "Where are they? Tell me!" Tommy elbowed his brother in the ribs. "Oh, please! She wouldn't know where they are! Do you seriously believe in this woman?" "Hey, I heard that!" The woman snapped, frowning. "I do know where your parents are...but my memory is very cloudy at the moment. Let's go back to the tent and I'll look into my crystal ball." "Look into your what?" Tommy asked, incredulous. He cracked up laughing. "Do you have a broomstick, too?" The lady turned and she grabbed Tommy's ear lobes and pinched. Tommy shrieked in pain. "You seem to have quite a smart mouth on you young man, so why don't I have you sleeping outside my tent with my dog Bumpkin?" "Bumpkin? What a funny name!" Tommy cracked up laughing hysterically. The woman let go of his ear lobes and stormed off into the distance. The four of them wondered out of the carnival and walked a short distance down the street and soon they were welcomed into a huge tent. The lady started laying out some cookies onto a plate and some juice. "Here, drink up. All of you. You poor dears. Must be very thirsty!" She started looking through her piles of clothing and then looked under her table before yelling out excitedly. She brought a round crystal ball and wiped the dust off it using a red cloth. She looked deeply into it, rubbing it gently. Tommy snorted and tried not to choke on his juice as the woman started to chant to herself. The ball began to glow slowly and colorful images began to appear in the crystal ball. Tommy dropped his glass of juice. "Wow! Cool! So this ball does work after all!"

The gypsy woman went on gazing deeply into her crystal ball, caressing it like it was her new born child, that unsettling fierce look of deep concentration never once left her face. Tommy's excited smile faded as he observed the woman. "So what do you see? Do you see anything at all?" The woman abandoned her gaze and flashed Tommy a stern look. "On top of being cheeky, you're also very impatient! Can't you see that I'm concentrating here? This isn't fast magic you know! You have to ask questions, and wait for the answers..." "Fine, ok then. So, ask questions and tell me what you see," Tommy demanded impatiently. "Tommy, take it easy ok?" Chikery scolded, "we're very lucky to have a place to stay for tonight and so let's not blow our chances and being kicked out into the streets!" The gypsy nodded and smirked. "What a wise brother you've got here. You can learn a damn thing or two from him!" She said, flashing a pointed look at Tommy. She went back to gazing at her crystal ball for several minutes while Tommy shifted from foot to foot. "Ahhhhhhhh....I see, I see....Yes, hmmm. I see it alright," the woman cried out excitedly. "What? What? What is it that you see?" Tommy asked hysterically. "I see, ok, that your parents and some other stranger too," the woman informed mysteriously, "Yes, I do see them very clearly in fact. Your parents and some other man, together. They're trapped. Inside a ball." Tommy and Chickery stared at each other in disbelief and then glared at the woman. Unable to control himself, Tommy cracked up laughing crazily, clapping his hands together. "They're trapped inside a ball? Like, you mean...that crystal ball of yours?" "I see nothing funny about this," the woman snapped coldly, "this is very serious business I'm talking about here! Your parents are trapped inside this ball, and they need air as soon as possible! I can see them now...very thirsty and they're nearly dying! We must go find them now!" "And where are they exactly?" Tommy asked, "the North pole?" "Listen, I feel a great sense of danger for your parents and so we must go right away! Follow me!" The woman instructed, getting up abruptly and slipping into a thicker coat before disappearing outside while the two brothers and Wilbert followed closely behind. "But it's getting late at night! Where are we going?" Tommy wailed. "You leave the finding to me, I know where they are! Oh, no. I need my crystal ball in order to find the location!" The gypsy ran back into the tent and Tommy rolled his eyes and snorted. "Great, we're stuck out here with a madwoman who looks into crystal balls and thinks she can find our parents!" The gypsy quickly ran out cuddling something underneath her coat. She walked over to the side of the road and got her car keys. She opened up all the doors. "Quick! All of you inside right this instant! We need to go right away!" The three of them bundled up into the car and closed the door while the woman slipped inside and tried to start up the car. The engine started slowly before dying down. "That's funny, I thought I've already filled up the petrol this morning," she muttered, frowning. "Hmmm, I think I must've forgotten!" Tommy and Chikery collapsed into their seats and covered their faces in agony. The woman tried once more and the engine started successfully and she cried out triumphantly. Great, lets get this journey on the road," Tommy muttered dryly. "Let's just focus on finding mom and dad, ok?" Chikery asked tiredly, closing his eyes and trying to drift off to sleep.

The ride turned out to a lot longer than Chickery had thought it would be and it was by far the most uncomfortable judging by the endless sharp turns and the bumpy ride thanks to the gravel on the road.

Chickery felt nauseous and had a bad headache was pounding away and it took all his strength not to end up hurling in the car.

Tommy, on the other hand, was living up to his reputation as a royal pain due to his constant shifting in the car and even Wilbert was getting restless, darting back and forth endlessly. The kitten meowed sadly and when the two brothers ignored him, it began to crawl onto Tommy's lap and from there it started to claw into him frantically. "ok, ok. Enough already!" Tommy cried out in annoyance, brushing Wilbert off. "Are we there yet? We've been on the road for ages now!"

Chickery rubbed his forehead. "Tom, just give it a rest ok I'm sure we're almost there." "Don't worry, we're almost there kiddies!" They gypsy announced merrily, driving over a pile of gravel on the road and the car bounced from side to side violently. "Geez, I sure hope so," Tommy muttered grumpily while Tommy turned green.

The car suddenly took an unexpected sharp turn to the right and all of them cried out in shock. Just as Chikery was about to lose control and puke onto the floor of the car the woman did another swerve before coming to a stop. She killed off the engine and excitedly got out. "That's it, kiddies! We're here!" "Thank goodness for that!" Tommy muttered and scrambled out of the car while Chickery got out and puke onto the ground. "Do I hear somebody sick?" The gypsy asked, fishing out her crystal ball and rubbing it, "You poor dear. Well, your parents are here somewhere in these dark woods."

She rubbed the ball constantly, frowning. "Why isn't this working now? I can't see messages at all! This is not good!"

"Oh great, so we came all the way out here and now it's for nothing!" Tommy cried hysterically. "Silence!" The woman demanded, flashing Tommy a dirty look. "Good things come to those who wait! ok now, let's take another look...hmmm, yes. I can see something now. Ahhhh...ah-huh!"

The gypsy grinned at the two boys. "I know exactly where they are! We're going down to the lake to find the ball! Apparently they're trapped inside!"

"Oh, no. Not more walking!" Tommy wailed. "But I've walked all day!"

The gypsy walked over to the car and got out a torch light from the glove compartment. "Well, nobody's forcing you to go. But I see your parents are having trouble breathing and so we need to release them right away!"

"well, where exactly are we supposed to find this ball?" Chickery asked in confusion.

"Ahh, see this is where I come in!" The gypsy exclaimed, her face lighting up. "I've consulted my crystal ball and it says that your parents are trapped in this creek not far from here! So we better get a move on immediately! Time is running out! We need to get to them soon or else they won't survive. They've been trapped inside this ball for days bow and needs air!" "Don't tell me we're walking again!" Tommy wailed, "my legs are hurting! Besides, we've been running all day, trying to get away from the lion can't you just drive your car over to where ever it is that you think our parents are?" " .at the creek," the gypsy finished the sentence, a haulty look on her face, "sure. I suppose I can if you're strong enough to carry both your parents and your brother back to my car because there's not enough petrol, the engines' nearly empty!"

Chickery sighed. "Fine. Alright then, we'll walk. Hopefully it isn't too far!" The four of them began walking off into the distance, with the gypsy as the leader while she flashed her torchlight from side to side in the darkness. Wilbert meowed out loud and it sounded like it was shrieking. Tommy's scooped it up into his arms and began to pat it soothingly while Chickery was having trouble following from behind.

He stumbled various times and by the time he got up he quickly fell back down a gain. The gypsy turned and shined her flashlight on Chikery. "Don't go hurting yourself ok? Be careful. We have a crises going on here and I can't carry you, I'm way too old!" "But he's blind!" Tommy declared angrily. "So somebody have to assist him!" "He's blind?" The gypsy asked incredulously, "why didn't you say something in the first place?" She took hold of Chikery's hand and guided him into the muddy creek and she let go of him.

"Alright. We're here kiddies. This ball is in here somewhere in the filthy water!" "I'm not going anywhere in there yuck!" Tommy cried in disgust, backing away.

"You don't have a choice. We're all going in there together!" The gypsy snapped.

Before anybody could protest, she pushed the brothers and Wilbert into the filthy water. And then hesitantly entered the creek herself.

The brothers rose from the dirty water and coughed, spitting out the filthy water and thrashed their arms frantically. "This water is disgusting! It stinks!" Tommy yelled out while Chikery and Wilbert struggled to stay afloat. Tommy suddenly noticed a gruesome, disgusting ball floating near by in the water and the ball was coming right at him!

"What the hell is that...that...thing?" He hollered. The gypsy's eyes lit up excitedly. "That's it! That's the ball I'm talking about! Your parents are inside! Quick, grab hold of it now before it gets away!" Tommy winced in disgust. "You cannot be serious! This thing here? It can't be!" The woman splashed water into the air in frustration. "I say grab hold of it! Your parents are inside and they're depending on you!" Tommy hesitantly got hold of the ball and nearly dropped it when he felt the slimy texture of it. He swam to the edge of the creek and got out, grasping onto the ball as he climbed out. By the time he got out of the creek he couldn't control his disgust over the ball and dropped it on purpose. The ball bounced up and down several times and he shrieked in horror. "Somebody out there? Help us! Please, help us!" A muffled voice rang out from inside the ball. Chickery gasped when he recognized that it was his own mother's voice. "Oh, goodness! It's mom, Tommy! So it's true, mom and daddy is in there!" "That's what I've been trying to tell you all along, thank goodness now you both believed me!" The gypsy exclaimed, getting out the creek and draining the water out of her blouse while Chikery and Wilbert did the same. "Now, let's not waste time and get a move on here! We need to get that ball to open! Come join me!" All four of them got together in a tight circle around the ball and they grasped onto it and pulled. They were amazed by the gross texture of it, the outside of the ball stretched like uncooked bread dough and with a sharp pull the gross outside skin of the ball snapped off and they fell to the ground. Tommy slowly got up and turned to stare at what was inside the ball and gasped when he saw his parents, brother Jake and another man he did not know lying together in a heap. To his horror, he realized that they were breathing heavily and that their faces were pale green. "Something's wrong with them!" Tommy yelled out frantically.

The woman came crawling over and she shook her head. "Yes, something is wrong! They aren't breathing properly! I think we're too late!" "No, no! Don't say that!" Chickery cried out angrily. "Surely, we can do something!" "I need to get back to the car right away," the gypsy replied in a panicked tone. She got up and ran off into the woods while the three of them remained rooted in place, staring helplessly at their family lying on the ground. Within minutes later, they glared up and saw a trail of bright lights shining directly at them and the gypsy drove the car towards them. She got out and started helping the brothers carry their parents and brother, along with the stranger into the back of the car.

All of them breathless, they jumped into the car and Tommy groaned at the weight of Chikery and Wilbert on his lap in the passenger seat as the woman drove out of the woods and onto the main road. The two brothers felt quite worried as the car bumped through out the whole journey and by the time they reached the hospital in one piece, Chikery realized that the woman had lied about the car running of petrol but he dismissed the idea and tried on focusing on the well being of his family in the car.

Tommy ran inside and informed that there was an urgent emergency and in a short while, they had people lifting his family members onto stretchers and loading them inside the hospital. All four of them stood in the long corridor, pacing endlessly. Tommy turned and hugged his brother. "I'm so glad that you're alright now, hopefully our parents and Jake would be ok too."

"Yeah, I'm glad everything's turned out ok," Chickery said, "but the worst is not over yet. I still can't see anything, and may never see again! And then there are our parents..." The gypsy turned to the two brothers and stopped pacing. "Actually, there is something you could do and it's guaranteed to help get your eye back and help your parents back to recovery...but it wont be easy let me just tell you that..." "oh, I'll do anything!" Chickery insisted excitedly, "I'll do anything just to get my eyesight back and for my family to be ok! Tell me on what I have to do to make things get better!" The gypsy took a deep breath. "As I've said to you, it isn't going to be as easy as you may think, ok? Things aren't going to happen right away because you need to do something nice for Larry, and as unbelievable as this may sound, you need to forgive him despite after everything he'd done to you. As mentioned, none of this is easy and so...", Chikery couldn't believe his ears, he was hoping the woman was joking but realized that she wasn't. "You cannot be serious! What kind of plan is this anyway? I can't find it in myself to forgive him, not after all the nasty things he'd done to me and my family! I can't forgive him, and most definitely I can't even think of doing anything "nice for him!" "You're too young to have all these feelings of anger inside of you," the woman explained softly, "in order to live a happy life you need to forgive and forget, it's hard but you must try. See, Larry is one good example. He's a very angry person, quite bitter towards the world. But that's because he didn't have a good relationship with his parents and his siblings! He felt very different and ignored. He felt like he wasn't loved by anybody and his father always judged him on everything he did very negatively and so that's why Larry ran away...and ended up being captured for the zoo." The brothers stared at the gypsy woman in astonishment. "How do you know all this about Larry?" Tommy asked. The woman cracked up laughing. "Trust me, I'm not just some mad woman who looks into my crystal ball all day! I can see the future you know, the ball's only there for guidance at times. Anyways, I really think you should do something nice for Larry, and find it in yourself to slowly forgive him. It's the only way sweetheart." Chickery sighed and didn't reply. His insides were full of hate and anger that he felt for Larry, after all that's happened but part of him could relate to how Larry felt, feeling like he was different and he did felt sympathy for Larry. Chickery felt an idea coming to him as he thought over Larry's situation with his family. "I think we need to go find Larry's father. It's time these two resolve some of their issues and learn to love each other again but...how can we go about finding his parents?" The gypsy smiled approvingly. "oh, honey. That is wonderful. I love the idea of yours, really do. And leave all the findings to me. That's why they invented the white pages, sweetie! You all stay here while I go ask for the book, ok?" The brothers went on hugging each other and they included Wilbert into the embrace while they woman d The four of them waited by sitting down in chairs and tried reading magazines to pass the time but soon enough Wilbert started to doze off in Chikery's lap and others yawned. Suddenly, a large collection of lions entered the corridor and the staff at the receptionist stared and gasped.

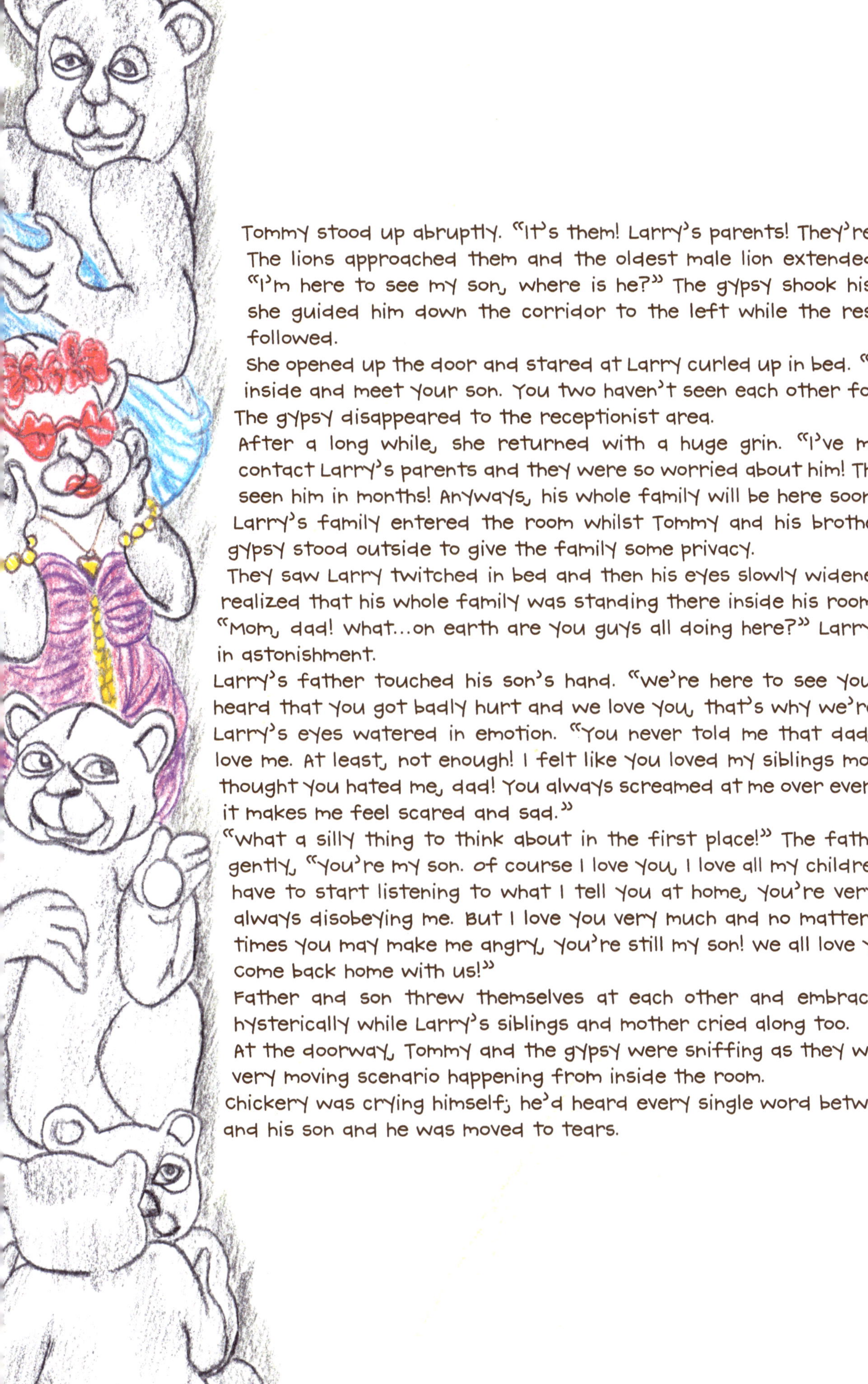

Tommy stood up abruptly. "It's them! Larry's parents! They're here!"
The lions approached them and the oldest male lion extended his hand. "I'm here to see my son, where is he?" The gypsy shook his hand and she guided him down the corridor to the left while the rest of them followed.

She opened up the door and stared at Larry curled up in bed. "Come right inside and meet your son. You two haven't seen each other for ages." The gypsy disappeared to the receptionist area.

After a long while, she returned with a huge grin. "I've managed to contact Larry's parents and they were so worried about him! They haven't seen him in months! Anyways, his whole family will be here soon."

Larry's family entered the room whilst Tommy and his brother and the gypsy stood outside to give the family some privacy.

They saw Larry twitched in bed and then his eyes slowly widened when he realized that his whole family was standing there inside his room!

"Mom, dad! What...on earth are you guys all doing here?" Larry cried out in astonishment.

Larry's father touched his son's hand. "We're here to see you, silly. We heard that you got badly hurt and we love you, that's why we're here."

Larry's eyes watered in emotion. "You never told me that dad, that you love me. At least, not enough! I felt like you loved my siblings more than I! I thought you hated me, dad! You always screamed at me over everything and it makes me feel scared and sad."

"What a silly thing to think about in the first place!" The father scolded gently, "You're my son. Of course I love you, I love all my children! But you have to start listening to what I tell you at home, you're very naughty, always disobeying me. But I love you very much and no matter how many times you may make me angry, you're still my son! We all love you, Larry. Come back home with us!"

Father and son threw themselves at each other and embraced, crying hysterically while Larry's siblings and mother cried along too.

At the doorway, Tommy and the gypsy were sniffing as they watched the very moving scenario happening from inside the room.

Chickery was crying himself; he'd heard every single word between father and his son and he was moved to tears.

oddly enough, he now understood why Larry was a jerk in the first place and he felt no more anger inside of him. He understood why Larry was the way that he was from the start now, after hearing the private conversation between him and his father.

Chikery felt the darkness in his yes slowly began to fade away and he started seeing the room in blurred colors for several minutes before he could see the room in normal sharp vision.

Chikery touched his eyes and gasped. "I can see! I can see again!" Tommy gaped at him and then cried out in excitement and he hugged Chickery. "oh gosh, I'm so happy for you!"

"well done sweetheart," the gypsy praised, smiling. She hugged Chikery briefly. "You got your vision back because deep inside you've forgiven Larry, well done!"

Suddenly a nurse came bustling up to them all breathless. "oh, thank goodness you're all here! Are you the children of Richard and Denise?"

"Yes, we are. So what's happened?" Tommy demanded in fear, "is my parents ok? Are they...hurt?"

The nurse smiled. "No, no. Nothing like that. Quite the opposite in fact. They have woken up, and so did the other boy...I take it he's your brother? And the other man must be your uncle? He's fine too. They all just had woken up! You can go see them now, but for a short time only, they're still weak."

Tommy hugged his brother and cried. "Thank goodness they're ok!"

The gypsy shrugged. "well, looks like my work here is done. Good luck to all of you. I better be going but I'll send you an expensive bill later for all of my services..." Chickery froze. "what bill? what are you talking about?"

The gypsy smiled mischeviously. "I did an awful lot for you and your family sweetie. But nothing in life is free. You need to pay up later, but don't worry I'll give you the bill for all that you owe me!"

She smiled and walked off out of the hospital while Tommy and Chikery gazed at each other green faced.

But they took several deep breaths to calm down. They had each other and now their family had survived. They'll just worry about the bill later. The two brothers walked off down the corridor to their parent's room, their arms around each other.

www.ingramcontent.com/pod-product-compliance
Lightning Source LLC
Chambersburg PA
CBHW042135120726
47911CB00022B/62